The Things You Cannot See

Sam Vickery

Copyright © 2019 Sam Vickery

First published worldwide 2019

All characters and events in this publication are fictitious and any resemblance to real persons, living or dead is purely coincidental.

All rights reserved.

No part of this publication may be reproduced, stored in a retrieval system or transmitted, in any form or by any means, without the prior permission in writing of the author.

www.samvickery.com

For Christine. Because when it comes to mother-in-laws, I got the best one.

Chapter One

Megan

"Megan?" Nate's voice called through the crowd of Sunday shoppers. I ducked behind a bookshelf, peering around it to see where he was, spotting him a little way ahead of me, Toby wriggling in his arms as he wrangled the pram and strained his neck to look for me. I should have called out. Smiled and waved and dashed to catch up to him. Taken Toby from him and settled the meltdown I could see already brewing in the overtired toddler.

Instead, I stepped back, heading into one of the perfectly set up nooks, displaying the kind of bedroom you too could have if you bought the carefully thought out Ikea design. I moved through the bedroom scene slowly, my fingers grazing against a sheepskin throw, my flat black boots scuffing against the laminate. A young, giggling couple came hand in hand into the room, ignoring me completely as they climbed onto the bed, bouncing up and down to test the mattress, cracking private jokes. I felt like a peeping Tom. Like a stranger who'd snuck into their bedroom, waiting for them to arrive. I watched their happiness with a mixture of confusion, jealousy and resentment. The woman bent low, kissing the man slowly and I fought the desire to throw something at them. We were in a department store, not a bloody nightclub.

Silently, I ducked through an archway and walked through another bedroom setup, then another, every step taking me further from my family. I arrived at one which had a high backed armchair placed by the fake window, a glossy scene of a city skyline at dusk pasted on to the perspex to create the illusion of a view. Purple and orange streaks slid behind black silhouetted skyscrapers. I glanced behind me checking I was alone, then climbed into the chair tucking my legs beneath me, curling up as small as I could manage as I stared towards the backlit view. I didn't know what I was doing. Why everything seemed to have changed so suddenly and so very drastically.

Two weeks ago, I'd been the happiest woman on the planet. Thirty eight weeks pregnant with my second child, the gender a surprise, though everyone knew I was secretly dreaming of a girl. Nate was too, although he would never have admitted it. The pregnancy had been almost dreamlike in its smoothness. Three measly days of morning sickness right at the start, and even then I'd only felt a bit queasy and had to sit down for half an hour until it passed. I hadn't had any of the aches and pains I'd expected from my first time around.

With Toby, I'd struggled with back pain, waddling from place to place in grimacing slow motion as I neared my due date. He'd been just thirteen months old when we'd decided to try for a second baby, and when I'd seen those two little blue lines appear on the Tesco pregnancy test just three weeks later, I'd been nervous about how I would cope with a toddler to take care of along with the exhaustion of pregnancy. I had thought it would take longer to conceive. That we would have time to prepare.

But my worry was needless. It had been easy every step of the way. No headaches. Nothing too extreme in the hormone department. Loads of energy. And the constant feeling that I was the luckiest woman in the world.

Seven days ago, I had given birth to a dark haired, brown eyed baby boy. His arrival into the world had been just as smooth as the rest. Three hours of active labour, twenty minutes of pushing. No tears. No drugs, no complications. The midwife had handed him to me, wrapped in the same blanket I'd been wrapped in as a newborn. I'd kept it safe all my life, through my school days, getting married, moving house, I'd never lost it. It had been the first thing we'd used to snuggle our first baby in moments after his birth, and now, our final child, Toby's baby brother, would finish the line.

I could remember thinking that perhaps, after it had become too small to keep him warm, we would put it away for safe keeping, and one day I might pass it on to one of my sons for their own leap into fatherhood. One day I might walk into a room and see the sparkling, brand new eyes of my grandchild peering out from beneath the mint green lambswool. And its journey would continue.

Nate and I had shared a look when we'd seen it was another boy, a look that communicated a thousand words in the dim warmth of the birthing room. *It doesn't matter one bit. We're so lucky. He's exactly right for our family.*

He was pink and perfect and we'd named him Milo. We'd both been nervous when Jane, Nate's mother, had brought Toby in to meet him. Ready to stave off any jealous rages and feelings of rejection he might have. But there had been none of that. Toby had loved him instantly, had laid beside him, stroking his soft downy cheek with a look of reverence, his voice soft as he told Milo in his babbling, lispy voice that he was his big brother and that he would be so kind to him *foo evah.* Forever.

It had seemed so strange to see my baby boy, my firstborn already taking on the responsibility of his new role. And for a few days, it had felt as if all of my wishes had been granted.

Now though, I couldn't stop myself from replaying that old proverb my grandmother always used to tell me. *Be careful what you wish for, it might just happen.* I'd never understood what she meant. It sounded like pure nonsense, like the one my mum used to say when I was sulky. *Megan, don't you know, I want doesn't get?* What was the point in getting something if you didn't want it? Pointless gibberish. But now, I was beginning to feel like I knew exactly what my grandmother had meant. Because, something was wrong. Horribly wrong. And nobody but me seemed to be able to see it.

When we'd come to this very store just a month previously to buy a new changing mat and eat Swedish meatballs and choose candle holders we didn't need, picking up cake cases in rainbow silicone, I had pictured coming back next time, light and free, without the pregnant belly to block my progress through the aisles. I'd imagined how I would walk as a mother to two children. How I would smile confidently as I meandered through the store, a tiny newborn held close to my chest as Nate and Toby dashed around opening drawers and cupboards, climbing inside them to jump out at me with wide grins on their faces. I'd thought this life was what I wanted. I'd been so sure. But I'd been wrong. I wished I could have known then what I knew now. I would have drugged myself. Poisoned. Thrown myself in front of a truck. *Anything* to stop this baby being born. Because he shouldn't be here. I'd made a mistake and now everything was going to change.

"There you are," came a deep, male voice from above me. Nate was looking down at me with concern in his hazel eyes, one hand on the pram handle as Toby ran to the bed, scrambling to get up on it. There was a high pitched keening coming from the depths of the pram, a wail of pure desperation. "He's hungry," Nate said, pulling the wheels closer, running his fingers through his messy brown hair.

There was something pink and crusty on the collar of his sky blue shirt, and he looked ready to throw in the towel. This had been such a bad idea. "We couldn't find you, are you okay?" he asked, pushing the pram back and forth quicker now, his determined rocking having absolutely no effect on the unbearable noise coming from within. I nodded, though I was anything but. Nate put his free hand on my shoulder, squeezing lightly. "Is it too soon to be out? We can go back home. You can go and lie down in bed."

"Yes," I agreed, the word coming out in a whoosh of relief. "Let's go back. I'm tired." I stood up, walking past Nate, heading for the exit.

"Megan?"

I spun around, raising an eyebrow in question. "What?"

"You need to feed him first. The poor little fella is starving."

"Oh... oh, of course." I took a step back towards him, approaching the sound of the screams with caution. With shaking fingers, I pushed back the hood of the pram and stared down into the dark interior. I knew what I was expected to do. And I knew that if I told Nate the truth, he would laugh at me. He would never believe me. Never understand.

The cries slowed as I lowered my head and Milo saw me, a halting, shaky sob shuddering from his throat as I reached for him and put him to my breast. Nate guided me back to the chair, handing me a muslin to mop up the dribbles. The baby fed ferociously, every draw of his small little mouth creating painful spasms right through my breast. It had never hurt with Toby. It had never felt so unnatural.

"There, that's much better," Nate smiled, catching Toby as he bounced from the bed. He carried him across to where I sat and the two of them smiled down at me. "See Tobes, he's fine now. All he wanted was his mummy."

I stared down at the baby, finally meeting his eyes as he released his mouth from me. He stared up at my face and I wondered what he was thinking. I let my gaze slide away from his. Then I stood up, placing him back in the pram out of sight, taking Toby from Nate's arms and heading for the exit.

Chapter Two

Megan

I paused halfway down the stairs, lingering nervously as I heard the sound of voices coming from the living room. Who could be here at this hour? It was almost Toby's bedtime. I'd gone straight to my room when we arrived home, telling Nate to use the expressed milk from the freezer if the baby wanted another feed, making out that all I needed was a decent nap. I hadn't slept though. Not for a single moment. I couldn't seem to switch off my mind to the nightmarish thoughts that swam freely around it.

Was this normal? This fear? This feeling that something was so terribly off balance? Nate had poked his head around the door about two hours after we'd arrived home, but I'd heard him coming slowly up the stairs, heard the sounds of Milo gurgling in his arms. Before he'd reached the bedroom door, I'd had time to turn my back, close my eyes, slow my breathing. He'd waited, watching me quietly and then I'd heard him sigh and leave without a word, his footsteps fading as he returned to the living room to play with Toby.

I'd felt guilty then. It wasn't fair for me to expect him to do everything alone. It wasn't that he wouldn't cope. He would. Probably better than any other dad I knew. He always stepped up to whatever life demanded of him, but that didn't mean it was okay for me to take advantage, and I knew I was letting him do far more than his fair share right now. Nate had never been the type to shy away from a challenge, it was one of the reasons I'd fallen for him in the first place, six years previously.

I'd been going through a period of dissatisfaction in my life. Working as a sales assistant in a camping and trekking shop, but never going anywhere myself. I'd dropped out of college at seventeen, knowing even before I'd started that I would never use the drama A level I was taking, and feeling sure I was wasting my time. I'd only liked the course because we mostly got to mess around and eat chocolate under the pretence of rehearsing and learning lines. I'd never actually been interested in going to auditions or getting roles, so when it came close to exam time, I had left, knowing I was meant for something different. Something special.

Seven years after walking out on my education, I'd bounced from one pointless job to the next and still been no closer to discovering what this mystical calling would be. It had seemed like a sign when a box of leaflets advertising a four week group trek through the Himalayas was delivered to the camping store during one of my tedious nine hour shifts. I'd read it from top to bottom and thought, *Hey, why not?* It had seemed like the answer I'd been searching for.

I used my staff discount to buy my backpack, my walking boots and several layered and pocketed outfits which made me look the part, even if I'd never done anything that could resemble a hike in my life, then handed in my notice, hoping this was the start of something new for me. The truth was, I'd never walked more than a few miles before, and even that had been on flat ground. I was clearly biting off more than I could chew but I knew I had to try, so after six weeks of nervous anticipation, I swallowed my fear, donned my fleece jacket and boarded the plane.

When it touched down in Kathmandu, I followed the signs for arrivals, terrified that I would miss the spot to meet my guide and the rest of the group. But just as I was nearing the exit, fending off touts trying to manhandle me towards their taxis and porters trying to prise my heavy backpack from my shoulders, I saw the bright orange sign and the group of nervous, excited travellers congregating beneath it. Nate, four years my senior, with twinkling hazel eyes and back then with a bushy beard that made him look like an explorer, smiled as I introduced myself, squashing down my nerves as I shook hands and made small-talk. I later discovered that he worked for an up and coming IT company who frequently paid for their staff to go on what they liked to call "life enriching and mind expanding" sabbaticals.

That first day in Nepal was an absolute whirlwind. We climbed aboard a tiny plane to make our way from Kathmandu to Pokhara, from where we would set out on our journey. We arrived, tired and dishevelled and in desperate need of a cold beer and a hot shower, but there was no time to rest. Instead, we heaved on our backpacks and left the town behind with barely a second glance, before climbing through the foothills into what felt like another world. The sounds and smells changed from cooking and dust, car horns and cow dung, to clean fresh water running through the icy cold streams, wood-smoke swirling from the chimneys of the tiny huts we passed, birds singing in the trees above us, bread baking tantalisingly off in the far distance. I was utterly silent as I took it all in. Shell-shocked. And struggling.

That evening, after two hours of what I considered vigorous walking to bring us to the tea house where we would spend our first night, I massaged my blistered soles and asked our guide if every day would be this difficult. He burst into laughter, his rosy cheeks chapped from the cool mountain air, pillowing in a wide smile as he explained that from here on in, we'd be doing a minimum of six hours walking a day. This was just "an easy stroll," he chuckled as he walked off to chat to the owner of the teahouse. I wanted to pack it in there and then. Get on a donkey, head back down to the town where there were cars and restaurants and a way to get back home, because I *knew* I could not survive this trip. I didn't have the strength, either mentally or physically. I'd been an idiot to ever think I could do something like this. I'd all but made up my mind to leave the following morning, but then Nate had plonked himself down beside me, propping his sock clad feet up against the wood burning stove and within minutes, I had forgotten to worry about what tomorrow would bring.

I loved hearing him talk, the deep tones of his voice, the easy smile that was never far from breaking into a rich, rumbling belly laugh that I couldn't help but join in with. I loved that he didn't look at me like I would be a burden, with my stiff, unworn walking shoes, my pristine backpack that had been wrapped in cellophane up until the week before departure.

Nate's friendship proved invaluable to me during the month that followed. He never left me behind, despite the fact that I was clearly the straggler of the group. Every morning, he materialised by my side, taking my water bottles from me without so much as a word, sliding them into his own backpack so as to make it easier for me to climb the never ending steps cut into the rock, or to scramble across narrow paths with sheer drops which would prove deadly to the clumsy hiker.

Several times, his hand would dart out, grabbing hold of mine, steadying me before I could fall. His easy, relaxed attitude and quick laughter, buoyed me up when I felt like I couldn't manage another step, and somehow, I always made it to the camp for the night, though often I was just as surprised as the rest of the group to find myself there.

As the weeks went by, I became stronger. Fitter. Faster. I began to grow in confidence. To know that I could do it without Nate's help. His hand reached out less and less to steady me during the daily hikes. But during the evenings, when we would sit out under the stars, sharing a musky woollen blanket and a bottle of warm beer, talking without pause, then basking in comfortable silence, he would reach out again, his hand finding mine beneath the warm layers. Those were my favourite moments. By the end of the trip, there was no question that we would be parted. Something had started that neither of us were prepared to give up. We'd been together ever since. It all seemed so long ago now. So far away. Dreamlike.

In the silence of my bedroom two hours before, with the memory of wood-smoke and cold air fresh in the forefront of my mind, I'd forced myself to sit up, determined to go downstairs to my husband and children and do my bit. I knew just how tired he'd been since Milo had arrived, and I knew I was being selfish. Nate deserved more from me. He always gave so much and expected so little in return.

I'd been on the edge of the bed, my feet already touching the soft pile of the carpet when the sound of a baby's cry echoed through the house, my milk letting up without my command, soaking through my t-shirt, leaving a sour stench in my nostrils. I'd stripped it off, slid back under the duvet and squeezed my eyes tightly shut again, my hands clamped over my ears, though no matter how hard I pressed, I couldn't shut it out completely.

Now, hovering uncertainly on the stairs, my breasts throbbed, hot and hard and aching with the need to be emptied. I heard a loud laugh coming from the living room and my shoulders relaxed as I recognised it. It was Jane. Only Jane. Probably come to bring us a casserole and offer her support to her poor, overworked little boy.

The other mums at the toddler group always laughed when I complained about my mother-in-law, telling me they wished they could swap theirs for mine. But Jane was intense. She treated Nate like he was five years old, cooking for us several times a week so he didn't have to worry, despite the fact that Nate was actually a pretty good cook himself. Admittedly, I wasn't. I tried, and I got by with the few dishes I had figured out, but I was never going to be Nigella and I always got the distinct impression that Jane had counted that as a black mark against me. The fact that I couldn't suitably nourish her precious baby boy.

Jane lived two roads away, and was always popping round with a new shirt she'd bought for Nate, a book she thought he'd like, an apple crumble she'd made from scratch. I'd given up asking her not to just barge in without knocking. My complaints about privacy always went in one ear and out the other. *"But I'm family!"* she would laugh when she turned up just as we were settling down to watch a film. Or *"Don't worry, I've seen worse on Game of Thrones!"* when she'd walked in on us completely naked, making love on the kitchen floor a few months after we got married. She hadn't even left after that. Just quietly closed the door and gone in the living room to watch our television with the volume turned up a little louder than usual.

Nate would never hear a bad word said against her, and as the years had passed, I'd given up trying to establish boundaries. And I did have to admit, she *was* fantastic with Toby. She was patient and playful and he loved her dearly. But sometimes, I couldn't help wishing she'd loosen the apron strings just a smidge and give us some space. My breasts twinged uncomfortably again and I palmed them over my t-shirt, sighing. Pasting on a smile, I padded down the stairs and into the living room.

"Hi, darling," Nate said, as I walked into the room.

"You feeling better?"

I nodded, though it was a lie. "Yes. Thank you. Sorry about that, I don't know what came over me."

"Ah, it's to be expected, love," Jane said, smiling up at me from her place on the sofa. Milo was cuddled up against her ample bosom, her huge, pillowy arm supporting his head, as the other snaked around Toby's back. He leaned into her, sucking his thumb, the long day wearing on him now as his bedtime loomed closer.

Jane was dressed, as always, in one of the five fifties style dresses she owned. This one was a brown cotton, stiff from ironing, with dusky pink roses printed at intervals across it. She made them herself, never able to find anything to her taste in her size. She had once told me that she didn't feel she should have to wear a bin-bag just because she liked the odd slice of cake. Her hair was a soft light brown, cut in a fringed bob with a slight wave, and her lips were pink and full, always on the verge of smiling, just like Nate's.

I walked to the sofa, leaning down to kiss Toby on

the forehead and taking a seat beside him. He moved away from Jane, shuffling over the cushions towards me, leaning his little head on my lap and yawning. He grasped my wrist, playing with my bracelet, and I stroked his silky brown hair. It was exactly the colour of Nate's now. When he'd been born, it had been blonde, like mine. He'd got Nate's hazel eyes too. Milo was far darker, his hair almost black, his eyes a deep, smooth brown. It seemed I would be the only fair haired, blue eyed member of our family.

Jane continued to hold Milo without offering him to me and I frowned, wondering if she knew her behaviour was rude. I was so aware of him. Such a tiny little thing, yet I could feel his presence like a constant beat pulsing around me. Why didn't she offer him to me? Did she think I wouldn't give him comfort like she could? Did she believe she could take care of him better than me?

I ran my fingers through Toby's hair, anger building in my belly as I stared at my newborn in another woman's arms. I was jealous, I realised. Jealous that holding him came so naturally to her.

That she could laugh and smile and not be affected by the strange, intense energy that seemed to emit from his very core. She looked so at ease in his presence. But along with the jealousy, I was also undeniably relieved that she was here, taking charge, holding him close so that I didn't have to. There was a silent battle raging in my head, but as I sat there, still and calm and nodding along to the conversation between her and Nate, I was suddenly aware of something. They couldn't see what I could. They didn't understand.

Abruptly, and without full awareness of what I was doing, I lurched forward, taking hold of Milo, grasping him in my arms and bringing him to my breast, sighing in relief as he latched and at last the pressure eased a little. He gasped and choked at the river of milk, but I adjusted his position and he resumed his task. I looked up to find Nate staring at me, his eyes questioning, shocked.

"What?"

"I'm pretty sure Mum would have passed him to you, had you asked. You didn't need to attack her, Meg."

"Oh, did I? I'm sorry, I just – "

"Don't be," Jane cut in. "Believe me, I remember. It's a kind of madness, isn't it? That need to have them close to you. It's those hormones. Powerful things. And the love... oh it's the strongest thing in the world." She leaned across the cushions, squeezing my shoulder. "You're besotted with him. Of course you want to hold him, I really should have thought." She leaned back against the sofa, smiling. "I remember the first time I held you, Nate..." she continued, her voice turning fuzzy around the edges as I stared down at Milo.

That was it. What was wrong. The thing that was so different this time around. *Love.* I couldn't feel it. It had been there when he was born, I was sure of it. I'd loved him just as much as I did Toby. But now, all I felt when I stared down at him was fear and confusion. And the intense desire to put him down and go somewhere as far from here as I could possibly go, so I wouldn't have to see him again. It was shocking. Disgusting. There was clearly something wrong with me to think such a dreadful thing. But now that I had thought it, consciously, clearly, I knew it was true. I didn't love Milo. I wasn't sure I even liked him and I had to do something to change that. To bring back the right feelings. To fix this.

I forced myself to cuddle him more securely as he fed. To block out the pain of his mouth tugging at my nipple, to stroke my finger across his downy cheek. I tried to will myself to feel it. Love. Adoration. I knew that for some mothers it took longer. My friend Kimmy had taken three weeks to feel it with her daughter, Josie. She said the midwife had told her it was far from abnormal to take time to bond. It was becoming less and less of a taboo subject. Women were encouraged to speak up about it. To get support. But she had said that when Josie was born, it had felt like she was taking care of someone else's baby. That wasn't what I felt. Not at all.

I wished Jane would stop talking about the unconditional love of a mother for her child. I couldn't bear to sit here smiling and pretending, all the while, wanting to beg somebody to tell me how to send this baby back, because not only did I not feel an ounce of love for him, but I really thought I might actually hate him. He released my nipple, a burp escaping his lips as his head lolled back in a deep sleep. I wished my own mum were here. That I could ask her if there was something wrong with me. But she and my dad had emigrated from my childhood home in Kent to Perth, Australia, three years before Toby was born, and these days we weren't close enough for that kind of conversation. They were reliving their party days, enjoying their freedom, and barely found the time to send Toby a birthday card between trips to the beach and cocktail parties.

I hadn't missed them in a very long time, but now, I would have liked to have my mum around to tell me I wasn't cracking up. That this was just my hormones playing tricks on me.

"Bedtime now, Mama?" Toby asked quietly.

"Yes, my darling, it is." I stood up, wordlessly, passing Milo back to Jane. "I'm taking Toby to bed."

"I can do that if you want to spend time with the baby?" Nate said, already on his feet. I shook my head. "No, he's fine. He's fast asleep anyway. I want to do it." I smiled down at my toddler, realising with relief that nothing had changed when it came to my feelings for him. I loved him as much as I ever had. I scooped him into my arms and walked out of the room, feeling better with every step I took.

Chapter Three

Nate

"You'll let me know then, sweetheart?"

"Yes, Mum, I said I would, didn't I? I promise, I'll let you know if we need anything. I'm sure we'll see you tonight anyway, won't we?"

"Well, I *was* planning to pop by after work. I have some clothes for the boys. Just a few things I picked up on sale from the supermarket."

"Great. Well, I'll chat to you then. I have to go, Milo is crying."

"Love you, baby."

"Love you, Mum."

I hung up, feeling tense and stressed. The sound of Milo's cries always made my heart race and my palms sweat. There was something so frantic about it, his very survival depended on whether or not his pleas were heard. I knew it was a clever evolutionary design, the sound so horrible that even if you wanted to, you couldn't ignore it, but with Toby, it had barely been an issue. There were two occasions I could recall, when he'd gulped in too much air whilst breastfeeding and spent most of the night screaming with the pain of trapped wind. I'd had to insist on taking him out of Meg's arms at three a.m, guiding her weary head down to the pillow so she could rest after hours of trying everything she could think of to soothe him. She would have stayed up all night without a word of complaint, but I'd seen how her hands shook from exhaustion, how close she was to crumbling into tears.

I'd strapped the squirming, miserable newborn in the baby carrier against my chest, wrapped my heavy coat around the two of us and we'd gone out into the peace and darkness of the night, that special time when it feels as though the world belongs to you and you alone. I'd walked briskly down to the beach, heading out over the pebbles to walk parallel alongside the sea, the waves rolling softly in and out, soothing, distracting. It had taken an hour of wriggling, fidgeting and bawling before he'd finally brought up an enormous burp and his heavy eyes had immediately closed in a much needed sleep.

When I'd returned home, Megan had only been half asleep, unable to rest knowing her baby was in discomfort. She'd taken him from me the moment I came into the bedroom, tucked him under her arm and the two of them had slept peacefully until morning. It had been the same the second time he gave himself wind too.

Those two nights stuck in my mind because they were the only times I had heard Toby cry for more than a couple of minutes in his first year of life. Megan was selfless and instinctive as a mother. Watching her made me see a strength and determination I'd known she had in her all along, but she'd never found an outlet to be able to show what she was capable of.

Motherhood was it. It was what she was made for. From the moment Toby was placed in her arms, she changed, and for the better. She was no longer indecisive or doubting and self-effacing. She was powerful and strong and completely unapologetic about the fact that she was good at it. She always seemed to know exactly what he needed before I had even realised he was growing restless. As a new father, I was scared for the first time in my life, never knowing what to do or how to handle him without breaking his tiny bones, but Megan was brilliant. Now she was the one leading the way, showing me how to be a father. It was as if she had some secret instruction manual guiding her through every hiccup and cry and grimace.

He was never far from her, and more often than not, I'd come home from work to find the two of them taking a nap in our bed, cuddled up close, smiling even in the depths of sleep. I'd watched them sleep on more than a few occasions. It was fascinating. They were like one person, their movements interconnected.

Toby would stir, his arm reaching out into the thin air above him. Megan would shift in her sleep, bringing him closer, soothing his fears. Sometimes his tiny mouth would begin to root and suckle against her collarbone, and though to me it looked as if she never woke, she would gather him to her breast and after a moment I would hear the noisy suckle as he began to feed. It had been beautiful to witness her blooming and changing into this confident, radiant woman day by day.

Putting the phone back in its cradle on the table and picking Milo up, rocking him gently in my arms until his cries faded to a soft gurgle, I reflected on just how polar opposite things were this time around. I'd heard Milo cry more in the eight short days of his life, than I had in the whole of Toby's first year put together.

Megan hadn't bonded with him. That much was clear to me. Rather than run to scoop him up at the sound of his cries, she would disappear off as soon as he needed her, and I found myself having to tell her more and more often to do simple tasks like feed him, hold him even. It wasn't right. And I was pretty sure I knew the reason why.

Toby.

Megan was so besotted with her firstborn that the thought of loving another baby, taking her attention away from Toby was causing conflict in her mind. She felt guilty. It was patently obvious. Milo had been planned and wanted, but I knew that the hormones and reality of his arrival were taking their toll on her.

On top of that, I knew just how much she had pinned her hopes on having a daughter. She'd confessed to me halfway through the pregnancy that she was sure she was carrying a girl, and that she was glad because it meant that Toby wouldn't be replaced. He would never have the same sort of rivalry he would have with a brother. Toby would want to protect his little sister, not compete with her. But she'd been wrong about it being a girl. And though she had acted like it didn't matter, I couldn't help thinking it was part of the reason she was slow to bond with our new son.

Mum had told me that Megan just needed time, and more than anything now, she needed my support. She needed to be put in situations where she would have no choice but to bond with her new baby. Time without Toby around so she wouldn't be afraid of hurting his feelings. So far my attempts at orchestrating this had been without success. Megan had come up with excuses time and time again. But today, I wasn't taking no for an answer. I gathered Milo up in his blanket and murmuring soothing words to him, I carried him upstairs.

Pushing open the door to the boy's bedroom, I found Megan in the rocking chair, propelling it backwards and forwards in a movement that looked far from relaxing as Toby climbed on his toy garage, reaching up to get his box of puzzles from the shelf. The box was heavy and far too big for him to manage alone. "Tobes, wait," I gasped, darting into the room and grabbing it just as he got hold of the edge. I shifted Milo into one arm. "Let me help you, mate, this is really heavy. Meg, didn't you see him? He could have really hurt himself."

"What? Oh, no. Shall I help?" she said, getting to her feet, coming over to where I stood.

"I've got it now. Are you feeling okay?"

"Stop asking me that. I'm getting fucking sick of it."

I stared at her in surprise. "Okay..." I faltered. "I was only asking."

"I'm fine." Her hands fidgeted in the space in front

of her, her thumbs tapping quickly against the pads of her index fingers. There were dark circles beneath her eyes and despite the fact that she had only just given birth, she was looking gaunt around the cheekbones. Was it even possible for her to lose the baby-weight so fast? It didn't seem healthy to me.

Toby riffled through the box of puzzles by my feet, pulling one out and promptly scattering all the pieces across the carpet. Losing interest, he turned, picking up a teddy bear from a cushion beside his chest of drawers, holding its stuffed purple body against him gently.

"Anyway," I said, feeling apprehensive. "I thought maybe you might like some fresh air? You and Milo could go for a walk along the beach while I do something with Toby. We could do some painting, couldn't we, Tobes?"

"Yes, Dada!" Toby grinned, dropping the purple bear and running to take my free hand. "Now, Dada?"

"No," Megan interrupted. "I'm not going out there."

"It's a gorgeous day."

"No. It's too early, he's not ready. It's dangerous."

"What do you mean? He's not going to get ill, Megan. We had Toby out from two days old, and that was in the coldest week of winter. Remember the snow? And he was fine, wasn't he? Wrapped up in that lovely warm snow-suit. Milo's not going to catch anything from a walk along Brighton beach in the middle of October. It's not the Arctic for goodness sake, and anyway, aren't you always going on about how the antibodies in breast-milk protect babies? What could possibly go wrong?"

"I don't want to have a discussion with you, Nate. I said I'm not going. It's not safe."

"Meg," I pushed, not ready to give up on my plan. "Aside from twenty minutes in Ikea, you've been indoors for days. You need some fresh air, and so does Milo. We can all go together if you prefer?"

She shook her head, her fingers still tapping and I could see that she wasn't going to budge. "Okay," I conceded reluctantly. "Maybe not a walk then. How about just spending some time together here instead. You two need time to get to know each other. Why don't you chill out in bed and I'll bring lunch up for you? You can put a film on or something?"

"What about Toby? I can't just spend the day watching television. I've got things to do."

"I'll take care of everything. Me and Toby need some quality time. We'll be fine." I stepped towards her, placing Milo in her arms and she looked at him with wide eyes. "Meg, sweetheart," I said softly. "I know it's all different. It's a lot to adapt to. But you're good at this. You're a natural. You just need to give it time, let yourself fall in love with him. I promise, Toby isn't going to miss out."

She stared at me, and for the first time since I'd met her, I realised I had no idea what she was thinking. I couldn't read her expression at all. She looked down at Toby, who was pulling at my trouser leg in his keenness to get started with art and crafts, and with a sigh, she pushed past me and walked into our room.

I watched her go, letting out a breath, thankful that for once she'd taken the baby with her. Maybe this was the start of getting our family back on track. Of her coming back to us from this lost place she seemed to have fallen into. I smiled down at Toby. "Come on then, little one. Let's go and get messy."

Chapter Four

Megan

I couldn't relax. Not with Toby downstairs out of sight. I couldn't be sure if he was okay. If he was safe. I hadn't wanted to take the baby with me, but there was some relief in knowing that he and Toby weren't together. I couldn't help the constant nagging feeling that Toby wasn't safe with Milo. It wasn't something I could explain, I knew if I tried I would sound ridiculous, but I had this constant feeling that if I left them together, something really awful was going to happen. And Milo would be the cause.

I glanced at him, lying in the middle of our mattress as I paced back and forth in front of the window. What was it about this baby that made me so scared? Was it possible to be born evil? Was that what I was sensing? As his mother, I would know. Mothers always know the truth of their children. Like when Toby tried to smile when he had hurt himself, but I knew he really wanted to cry. I could always see it. But if Milo was bad, if there was something truly evil in his soul, why had he come to me? Did I deserve this? Had I done something to bring this to our family?

He kicked his legs and I looked away, my thoughts going to Toby again, wondering if he was okay without me. I dug my fingernails into my palm, squashing down the fear inside me. Nate would take care of him. He was a good dad, and a good husband. He only wanted the best for all of us. But he didn't know about Milo. He didn't seem to realise what was going on. The danger under our own roof. I could see already that he had fallen for him. He loved him.

"Stop it, Megan," I whispered harshly. "Stop these thoughts. It's just a baby. *Your* baby." I was overtired. Letting my fears spiral out of control. Telling myself stories that had no possibility of being true. Of *course* he wasn't evil. Of course my family was safe.

"Pick up your baby and hold him close," I commanded, bouncing nervously on my toes. I approached the bed slowly, my eyes trained on his face, my lungs burning as I held my breath. *This is crazy,* I thought, lowering myself to the mattress. I reached out to touch him lightly on the belly, and saw that my hands were shaking. He stared at me with those dark, chocolaty eyes, unlike mine or Nate's. "You're *my* son. You're only a baby. You can't hurt me," I whispered. Slowly, I lifted him into my arms, pulling him to my chest. "I have to take care of you. I know I do... but I don't know how. What is it about you, Milo? I don't understand you. Not one bit."

He gurgled, his hand reaching up to my cheek. His fingers brushed against my skin and I stared down at his face. "Just a baby. You're just a tiny baby," I whispered. I looked into his eyes, trying to make myself feel the right things, rather than this fear that seemed to consume me from the inside. "Milo," I whispered, stroking a finger through his dark tuft of downy hair. "My son, Milo. My baby."

The more I stared at him, the more terrified I felt. It wasn't working. I wasn't convincing myself of anything. I let out a gasp as I watched his eyes. They seemed to be changing second by second. The brown irises blurred and darkened, a brilliant red spreading from the pupil, over the iris, further and further outwards, the whites disappearing, transforming until there was nothing but empty scarlet eyeballs staring up at me. I screamed, dropping him onto the mattress, rushing backwards, stumbling over a pile of books at the foot of the bed, scattering them everywhere. "Keep away!" I breathed. "Stay away from me! You stay away from my family, do you hear me?" He let rip with an ear-splitting wail, and I scrambled back until I was pressed hard against the wall, crouched low in readiness.

The bedroom door swung open and Nate rushed in, looking from me to the screaming demon on the bed. "Megan? What is it? What happened?"

"The baby – there's something wrong!" Nate turned towards him and I stood up fast, consumed with panic, my hands outstretched as if I could stop him, though I didn't dare to go any closer. "Wait! No, don't touch him! Oh, please be careful!" He leaned forward, obscuring the thing from my sight. "Nate?" I asked, my voice shaky.

He straightened, Milo tucked safely in his arms. "He seems fine to me," he said, his expression questioning. Doubting. He tilted him in my direction.

"He's fine," he repeated. "What happened?" He didn't smile as he asked. His expression was cold. Judging. *He thinks it's my fault,* I realised, shocked at how easily he'd been manipulated by this tiny being. *He doesn't believe me. He doesn't see.*

"His eyes..." I said, shaking my head slowly, shocked that he couldn't see the issue. "What about his eyes, Nate?"

Nate looked at him, then back to me. "They're fine." He gave a shrug. "I don't understand, Megan? What am I supposed to be looking for?"

"I – he..." I stammered. I looked down at the carpet, away from his probing stare and sighed, not knowing how I could possibly explain without sounding like I'd lost my mind. I took a hesitant step towards them, and then another. Peering down, I saw that Milo's eyes had returned to their normal colour. He was clever. He didn't want Nate to see. I shook my head. "They changed back," I whispered.

"What?"

I looked up suddenly aware that Toby was missing. "Where's Toby? Where's my son? I have to check on

Toby."

"He's fine, Meg, he's making a card for Milo, to say welcome to the family."

I glared at him, furious that he'd put such an idea in his head. What a ridiculous thing to do. "I need to see him," I said abruptly. I walked out of the bedroom, leaving Nate with the baby before he could try and make me hold him again.

Chapter Five

Megan

The room is compressing around me. I feel as though I'm in an airtight chamber, the kind they lock-down to prevent fire, sucking the oxygen rapidly from the room to protect ancient documents. There is no escape. No mercy. I have to get out, and it's not because I'm afraid for my own safety. It's because I can feel what will come if I don't. I have to protect my child. He's in danger. He is being watched, all the time. And if I turn my back, if I shut my eyes, even for a second, that thing that everyone believes is just a baby, will strike. And I'll regret it for the rest of my life.

I woke suddenly, unable to breathe, my throat seizing as it spasmed painfully, trying to will itself into action. My head was rooted to the pillow, my arms prone at my sides. Perhaps this was what it felt like to go under anaesthesia. Aware, yet incapacitated. Stuck in the terror that there was no way of breaking free, that your body was no longer within your power to control. With a desperate gasp, I finally felt the relief of air filling my lungs, my body coming back to me. I sat bolt upright in one fluid movement, breathing rapidly until I was certain the apnoea had passed.

The room was dark and I could hear the muffled snores coming from beside me where Nate slept. I couldn't remember coming to bed. I had no recollection of putting Toby down or of feeding Milo.

Unsteadily, I swung my legs over the edge of the mattress, a hollow feeling in the pit of my stomach. A tiny green light blinked from the bedside cabinet, and I stared at it, uncomprehending for a second. I stood, confused, bending over the Moses basket, needing to check on the baby, yet not wanting to. The basket was empty. All at once, realisation dawned on me. I took two strides towards the blinking light, grabbing the small white box in my hands, holding it up to my face. The baby monitor. *The fucking baby monitor!* He'd put them in together. In Toby's room. How could he be so stupid?

Still gripping the smooth plastic monitor in my palm, I ran out of the bedroom and into the blackness of the hall. I hit my shin hard against something solid and looked down to see the silhouette of Toby's rocking horse pushed against the wall. It didn't matter. I didn't let it slow me down.

I reached Toby's bedroom door and swung it open, my skin prickling with fear. There was a soft red glow coming from the plug in night-light in the corner and it gave the room the appearance of a horror movie. How had I ever thought it was relaxing? I walked straight to Toby's toddler bed, crouching down beside him. He lay on his back, totally still, his eyelids almost translucent, and for a moment, I wondered if I might be too late. I placed a shaking hand on his chest and when I felt the slow rise and fall of his breathing, I balled my hand into a fist, digging my fingernails into my palm in relief, a smile breaking out across my face. He was okay. My sweet boy was safe.

Slowly, I stood. I turned towards the cot on the opposite side of the room and took cautious, silent steps until I reached it. Peering over the bars, I saw him. He too, was lying quite still, absolutely silent. Yet he wasn't sleeping. His eyes were wide open as he stared up at the ceiling. I lurched backwards, not wanting him to see me, wondering if he knew I was there. If he'd been waiting for me all this time.

I shuffled back until I was beside Toby's bed again, slipping my hand beneath his blanket to find his hand, holding his warm fingers between my ice cold ones for comfort. I felt sick with fear. My breasts ached, and I knew I needed to empty them, but I couldn't seem to find the strength to go to him. The courage to pick him up and feed him. And as long as he was silent, I knew I wouldn't be the first to break that spell.

Instead, I reached out and picked up a bright orange stacking cup from Toby's toy basket. I held it beneath my breast, massaging and kneading, collecting the milk that should have been for my son, sighing as the discomfort eased. I repeated the process with the other breast and put the cup down, finding Toby's hand again and squeezing it gently. I couldn't take my eyes off the cot in the corner of the room. No sound or movement came from within, but still, I knew he was there, that he was awake.

What could he be thinking right now? Was it normal for a baby to just lay silently, wide awake, not crying out? It seemed sinister to me somehow. I wanted to bring him back to my room so that he wouldn't be able to do anything bad to Toby, but the idea of picking him up stopped that plan in its tracks.

Instead, I twisted on the carpet and leaned my head into the edge of Toby's mattress, inhaling the scent of his warm skin, remembering the early days with him. It had been so different. So special. I'd been good at this. Mothering. Taking care of him. I *knew* I had. It had felt so natural to me, so easy, and I'd loved it. He was an easy baby, right from the beginning. He'd smiled so early, and I had felt reassured that I was getting it right. It was like he was speaking right to my heart. *"You're doing so well, Mama, I'm so pleased I got you."*

Nate had been happy too. He took on the role of keeping me fed and hydrated. He made me fresh vegetable juice, sweetened with apples and carrots, to keep my strength up. He took charge of the housework so I could concentrate on feeding and taking care of Toby. He had walked around with a dazed expression of pure joy and pride and gratitude on his face, and I had wondered why we'd waited so long to do this. To become a family.

This time, though, it was so different. So horribly wrong. And as I looked at the unvaccumed carpet, the toys thrown haphazardly around the edges of the room, the pile of laundry overflowing from the basket, I knew it was all my fault. I was failing. Somehow, though I had thought I'd found the one thing I could do with confidence, I was fucking it up. What kind of mother is afraid to touch her baby? What kind of person would rather syphon her breast-milk into a dirty cup than use it to nourish her child? I felt lost and confused, but more than anything, I felt terrified. And I knew that Nate didn't understand. Would never understand.

The truth was, Milo hated me. I could feel his anger bubbling away inside him. And it was for me, all for me, because somewhere along the line, I'd let him down and got something wrong. It was *my* fault he was like this. Of course it was. If a child is bad, who else is there to blame but the mother? I wished I knew how to fix it. How to go back to before. How to remember what I did to be that perfect mother everyone aspired to be like. But I could not seem to find my way back. I couldn't drag myself out of the darkness. And everyone would suffer all because I had failed.

I pulled myself up to standing, needing to do something, to keep moving and stop the thoughts from swirling and poisoning me from within. I went around the room, collecting toys, putting puzzles back in the right boxes, grabbing a pack of baby-wipes and cleaning every surface, shelf, plug socket, treading carefully, never getting close enough to the cot to be seen. I scrubbed at the skirting boards, wiping away the layers of dust and grime that had collected, piling the dirty wipes in a heap as I discarded them, grabbing fresh ones from the packet.

I scooped up the laundry and took it down to the washing machine, taking the steps two at a time, knowing I shouldn't leave the boys alone together for long. But I *had to* do this. I had to keep the house tidy. It was the first step, to getting back on track. To being the mother and wife I wanted to be. I grabbed the dustpan and brush from the cupboard under the stairs, and dashed back to the boys, checking Toby again, staying out of sight of Milo. I could hear his breathing had become heavy now and I was sure he was sleeping, but still I couldn't bring myself to look.

I got down on my hands and knees, and with fast, determined strokes, I swept the carpet from corner to corner. When I'd finished, I emptied the dustpan into the bathroom bin and returned, repeating the process all over again. I felt like there was electricity running through my veins, like I was superhuman somehow. If I wanted to, I could keep going forever. I was powerful. I didn't need to rest and it wasn't safe to sleep. I could survive fine without it. So many mothers did. Why not me?

I could protect my family if I just kept going. I could prevent Milo from destroying my world.

Chapter Six

Jane

I hummed softly under my breath as I adjusted the soft fleece blanket around the tiny sleeping bundle in the Silver Cross pram, smiling as I ran my fingers over the ridged cream handlebar. The pram had been bought for me by my own parents back when I'd become a mother myself. They'd found it second hand in a charity shop, a steal even in the eighties before vintage had been so in fashion as it was now. At the time, I'd thought how dated the fifties model was in comparison to my friend's newer ones, but I'd quickly grown to love it and somehow it had withstood the test of time and was as sturdy today as it had ever been.

I loved the huge heavy blue hood, the cosy interior where a baby could stretch out and be comfortable even as they grew into a chubby, wriggly toddler. So much more freeing than these new buggies and pushchairs with their complicated straps and twenty different ways to tilt and angle the seats. I never felt like it was safe to press those levers, not with a fragile baby strapped to the chair. I always feared that they might suddenly be catapulted into the road. But then, I supposed, that's what all those straps were for.

I'd kept the Silver Cross in my loft hoping to see it in use again someday, and when I'd found out that Megan was expecting, I hadn't hesitated in offering it to her for my first grandchild. I'd longed to see a brand new baby in it again. To remember. She'd never refused me directly, but Nate had hedged and dodged whenever I brought the subject up, and one day, when Megan had been around seven or eight months gone, I'd walked into their house to find a brand new three in one travel system blocking up their entire hallway. I'd never mentioned it again.

But there was a silver lining. I'd kept it for myself and as soon as Megan was happy to have him out of her sight for a little while, any time I got the chance, I would take Toby out for long walks along the seafront, smiling down at him as he cooed and gurgled from his warm little nest.

Now I took Milo on the same well travelled path

as I'd taken with his brother so many times. It was cool this morning, a nip in the air and my cheeks stung as the wind whipped my hair into my eyes. I swept it back off my face, securing it with a hairband, ignoring the way people paused to stare at me.

It was always the same. The wide mouthed toddlers, pointing up at me with sticky fingers as they pulled at their mummy's jumpers, exclaiming, "Look at that fat lady, look, there she is!" or "Mama! That lady is enormous!" I would purse my lips, pretending not to hear as the mothers blushed and shushed and ushered them away in the opposite direction. Worse than that were the mean comments. The teenagers shoving into me as they passed and making cruel jokes, not bothering to lower their voices. The tuts as I queued unashamedly to buy a cone of chips or an ice-cream. As if they had more right than I did to be there. As if I should be disgusted with myself.

I never acknowledged a single comment. Not ever. I saw a couple whispering now, heads together as they watched me from the bench, pointing and giggling, and I continued to walk, slow yet steady, head held high.

It wasn't that it didn't affect me. That their judgement wasn't a constant source of discomfort and annoyance in my life. But having endured the cruelty and curiosity of people for so long, I'd eventually grown numb to it. It was like I was constantly wearing a heavy suit of armour. Their weapons banged and crashed against me, irritating, disturbing my peace, but they couldn't pierce my skin. They could never sink deep into my flesh and cause the pain they might once have done. I'd been called far worse names than fat.

Milo stirred in his sleep, sucking at the air and I realised there was a good chance he would wake for a feed soon and I had nothing with me. It had all been a bit of a rush. The dawn phone call from Nate, hopping out of bed and throwing on some clothes to go and meet him at the park. I'd arrived at the playground in the early morning mist to see him in the distance, pushing Toby in the swing with one hand, rocking Milo in the cradle of his free arm and looking ready to collapse.

Usually I loved catching him in these candid moments. My baby boy all grown up and making me so proud with everything he did. He was such a good father. I loved snapping pictures of him smiling at Toby as he read to him, playing with Milo's little toes as he changed his nappy. But today, I hadn't taken pictures. I'd seen the desperate, aching exhaustion on his face as he tried to soothe the baby. The way he took deep breaths into his lungs as if he were summoning all his strength to get through each and every moment.

Megan wasn't there. Again. It was fast becoming a habit, and one that would cause friction in her marriage if it continued for much longer. Her absence was becoming the norm and it was clearly taking it's toll on my poor Nate. I both resented her for it, and at the same time, was filled with empathy for her, remembering my own, not insignificant struggles as I adapted to being a parent.

There is a sense of helplessness you can never escape when you are a parent, when you realise you can't fix everything for your child, no matter how much you might want to. That despairing feeling of wanting to tuck them away safe in your arms, yet having to step back, to let them figure it out for themselves. Even now, it was something I struggled with daily. And I wasn't blind to the fact that I often failed. Meddled. Did more than any other mother I knew, yet still, it never seemed enough. Which was why, I had walked straight over to Nate, hugging him tight before telling him to pop into the twenty-four hour supermarket and buy brunch for himself and Toby to eat in the park, and I'd taken my newborn grandson into my arms and walked away.

He needed a break from the tears. And if I was honest, I wanted Milo to myself, just for a little while. Every time I held him, I could feel the tension pouring from Megan. Even when she wasn't looking at me, I knew she was far from relaxed. She was aware of everything I did, even when her eyes were fixed in the opposite direction. I wanted a chance to bond with Milo without an imaginary clock ticking away, making the experience tense and hurried.

I was in two minds about how to help her. Part of

me knew I needed to give her more space. To allow her to figure out this new stage in her parenting journey for herself. To make her own mistakes. She needed to get to know her son without me creating a barrier and I was aware of the fact that I would have to back off for that to happen.

But another part of me wanted to do so much more. To hold this baby so she didn't have to, to feed him, love him, comfort him in a way I wasn't sure she was capable of right now. Because I'd seen something in her eyes that frightened me, and no matter what, I *would* keep this baby safe.

Chapter Seven

Megan

The children were gone. Just seconds ago, I'd been deep in sleep on the rug beside Toby's bed. There were times in my life when I'd woken slowly, the light seeping in through the curtains, coaxing and gentle as it carried me back to consciousness. That was how you woke when life was good. When you didn't live in constant terror. I never woke like that now, not since Milo had arrived.

I hadn't meant to fall asleep. As far as I could recall, I hadn't even been tired. I'd been cleaning, and tidying and then when that was done, I'd paced. Back and forth, back and forth, like a sentinel in front of Toby's bed, as if I could protect him from anything that came his way. I'd felt like I could do it forever.

And yet somehow, moments ago I had found myself torn from sleep, on my feet and darting from one side of the room to the other, spinning in circles like a headless chicken, my brain still trying to grasp what was happening while my body sprang into action, coiled as if I may have to fight for my survival. I stood trembling and nauseous in the middle of the bedroom, staring at the empty, unmade bed. Toby was gone. And I didn't need to look in the cot to know that Milo was missing too. I could feel his absence.

I ran from the room and down the stairs, my heart thumping hard against my ribcage, my feet slipping against the polished wooden floorboards on the hallway floor. I threw open the living room door, darting inside then rushing out again as soon as I saw it was empty. I went to the kitchen next, skidding to a stop on the tiles as I saw my mother-in-law. She was sitting in the wicker chair by the patio doors, Milo tucked into her bosom, drinking noisily from a bottle.

Jane's eyes were misty with affection as she watched Milo feed, his fingers grasping the neckline of her dress, his eyes fixed on hers. My gaze widened as I saw the tin of formula on the kitchen side, the loose powder sprinkled messily over the surface. The steriliser was emitting a soft hum from beside the slow cooker, and I could see several dummies sitting on the top shelf of it.

The Things You Cannot See

Milo didn't use dummies, nor had Toby. And I'd made my views on formula perfectly clear to Jane in the past. She'd begged and moaned to be allowed to buy a few tins for her house so she could keep Toby with her for longer, maybe even have him overnight once a week, but I'd put my foot down. In fact, I'd gone completely overboard, telling her it was junk food for babies, designed for mothers who didn't care and who were far too lazy to step up and do their duties. I hadn't meant it. Not really. But I'd been incensed at the idea that she thought she could take my son from me if only she had a way to keep his tummy full. I didn't mind her having him for an hour or so, but he was *my* baby, not hers, and there was no way on earth I was going to let her relive her mummy days by playing dolls with *my* child. He needed me to be there for him, and I needed him too.

I couldn't imagine waving him off and forgetting all about him for an afternoon, let alone a whole night. As if I would have slept! It was out of the question, but Jane had been so persistent I'd had no choice but to leave no room for negotiations. If causing a massive scene about formula was the way to achieve it, I was only too happy to play the over-dramatic mother. I couldn't believe that after all we'd discussed, she would go out and buy formula for Milo now, without so much asking permission. I stepped forward, still breathless, and she looked up, her eyes meeting mine, a welcoming smile on her lips as if I hadn't just caught her in the middle of destroying my trust. "What the hell is this?" I demanded, gesturing to the tin. "And where's Toby?"

"He's with his daddy at the park," Jane replied softly. "And Milo is just falling asleep, so try not to shout, love."

"What are you feeding him? Surely not this?" I spat, ignoring her instruction not to shout. Who on earth did she think she was, telling me to be quiet in my own house? The cheek of it!

She gave a shrug. "Yes, that. It's one of the top brands, I checked on google. And Milo was hungry. I really didn't have much choice, Megan."

"There's milk in the freezer! *My* milk. The stuff that he needs."

"There isn't. He's got through it all, and you haven't topped it up. He's a newborn baby, Megan. He needs feeding regularly, and if you aren't going to feed him yourself, and you won't make the time to express regularly..." she shrugged again, sliding her eyes away from mine, and I got the sudden urge to punch her. "Jane, this isn't your decision to make! Did you even ask Nate? Or did you think you could just do what you wanted without considering our views on the matter? It's unacceptable Jane, can't you see that? You know my thoughts on this! Why didn't you ask me? I was only upstairs, for fuck sake!"

"Alright, alright, calm down. Really, there's no need to get hysterical over this, Megan. Honestly, you'd think I'd taken him out for his first tattoo the way you're hammering on. I didn't wake you because Nate said you'd had a rough night and you wouldn't wake up when he tried to talk to you this morning. I didn't think it was worth disturbing you for such a silly issue. It's *one* bottle. *One*. And he's barely had half of it, so if it means that much to you, come and take him and feed him yourself. He's still hungry and I'm sure he'd love to spend some time with you."

Her words were said in the most offhand manner she could muster, but I knew what they meant. She was throwing down a gauntlet for me. The words were innocent enough, but her eyes were hard, challenging. She *knew.* She could see the war raging in my mind. The struggle of wanting to do what was right for my son, yet having my skin crawl at the thought of holding him, touching him, having him suckle at my breasts, sharing such an intimate moment with him. It turned my stomach. Jane smiled up at me and I hated her too in that moment. It was as if a silent communication passed between us.

You win. You know I can't.

You're right. You can't. But I can. And I'll do it so much better than you ever would.

I hesitated so long that the decision was made for me. Milo released the teat, turned his head into her dress and gave a tiny snore. Jane gave a smug little smile as she patted his bottom. "Next time, maybe," she said. "You *do* look exhausted though, Megan. Why don't you go back to bed for a bit? I have the afternoon free, I don't mind waiting with Milo until Nate and Toby get home."

I stared at her, taking in the way she held the baby so close, the protective arm wrapped around him, the way she looked at him with such adoration. And all at once, it clicked. She could see what Nate could not. She knew the truth. What Milo was capable of. The evil he carried in his heart. But the difference between her and me was that *she* didn't care. She wanted him for herself, despite all that. It was so obvious. She *wanted* me to reject him so that she could have her turn playing mummy again.

She'd never really stopped, never let go of Nate, let him be an adult. She'd tried so hard to take Toby from me, but I'd held strong, our bond had been too powerful, she could never penetrate it. Never compete with what I could offer him. But she could see my weakness with Milo. And she wouldn't hesitate to take advantage of that.

I should have felt relief. Given him up to her so I didn't have the burden of his care to worry about anymore. But I couldn't. It wasn't as simple as that. I had to keep him close. With me, under my supervision. I didn't want to, but it was the only way I could be sure that he wasn't spreading evil in the world. Causing pain and suffering to other children. He was my burden, but that didn't mean I had to like it.

I nodded slowly, wanting nothing more than to run out of the room so I didn't have to speak to her anymore. "Yes..." I managed. "I think I will go back to bed for a little while. If you're sure?"

"Of course dear, you go and rest. Milo and I will be fine. Do you want to hold him before you go?"

"No. I don't want to disturb him."

"Of course you don't. There's pastries on the side, why don't you take one up with you? Keep your milk supply up?"

"No. Thank you. I'm not hungry."

She pursed her lips but didn't say anything more. I left her there, making a show of climbing the stairs, heading up for my nap. I opened and closed my bedroom door without stepping inside, then on silent footsteps I returned to the top step, lowering to my haunches, listening hard. I couldn't trust her. Not anymore.

The clock in the hall below ticked loudly, the minutes merging into one another. I shifted my position, aware of the tension in my muscles, the panic levels in my body on the verge of overspilling. Toby should have come home by now. Nate wouldn't keep him out this long. What if something had happened? What if I'd missed something while I'd been sleeping? Jane could have been lying about the park.

The letterbox clanged, making me jump, an envelope falling through it to the mat below. A handful of leaflets followed directly after and finally a small thin parcel. I heard the gate squeak closed as the postman moved on to the neighbours next door, the bark of their Alsatian as he rang their doorbell. Still I didn't move.

Finally, when I felt like I might run screaming into the street, and down to the park to find them myself, I heard the sound of a key in the door. I was moving before it was even open, running down the stairs to greet them. Nate stepped over the threshold, Toby grinning beside him and I was sure my heart might burst with relief at the sight of him, safe and healthy and happy. "You're back, you're okay," I cried, falling to my knees in front of him, pulling him to my chest, sobbing freely.

"Meg, we just went to the park. There's no need for the dramatic reunion," Nate said, slipping his arms free from his jacket. "I mean it, Megan, stop it. You're going to scare the poor boy." He reached down, disentangling Toby from my grasp and I held on tighter.

"No, don't take him from me, don't you dare!" I cried, tears streaming down my cheeks, mixing with snot and sweat and saliva.

"I'm taking him for a snack. For Christ sake, pull yourself together. You're a mess!" He yanked Toby into his arms, out of my reach and stalked off to the kitchen, leaving me in a crumpled heap on the doormat.

Chapter Eight

Nate

I carried the thick brown envelope into the kitchen, smiling. I'd forgotten it was coming, but now that it was here, I was sure it would spark something in Megan. Some primal, protective feeling which right now was squashed deep down inside her. I'd never understood the trend of having the birth of a baby documented, photographed and video-taped to look back on whenever you wanted. It seemed macabre to me, sitting down with a biscuit and a cup of tea to watch yourself go through the worst pain imaginable, to hear your own screams and relive the memory of nearly being torn in two.

To me, it was like asking someone to film you having your appendix out without anaesthetic so you could revisit it anytime. If it were me who'd been bellowing until my throat was raw, I would want to bury that memory in the recesses of my mind never to emerge again. It was hard enough to be the bystander. The useless birth-partner who could do nothing to make it better, who had to watch and endure and pretend everything was alright and it was all going just as it should, though in truth, I had no idea myself. Re-watching it all was not my idea of fun.

But Megan had insisted we do it with Toby and, I had to admit, when the screaming was over and the camera had panned in on Megan's flushed face as she cradled the life we had made together, I had felt the bizarre and unusual sensation of a tear sliding slowly from the corner of my eye and I had admitted silently that it was indeed beautiful. We'd hired the same company to document Milo's birth, and now I had in my hand the final edited film and the ten stills we'd asked for.

I made a pot of tea, the habit instilled in me by my mother who would never accept a bag in a chipped mug, and poured out a packet of custard creams, Meg's favourite, onto a plate. Balancing everything on a tray, I tucked the envelope under my arm and carried it all into the living room. Megan was sitting on the windowsill, staring outside into the distance through the sheer net curtains. She didn't look up as I put the tray on the table. Toby was down for his nap and Milo was in a little bouncy chair I'd forgotten we'd bought. I'd come downstairs after a disturbed night sleep to find everything out of the cupboard under the stairs, and Milo in the chair. We'd been given it for Toby when he was tiny, but Megan had declared it useless and unnatural. It seemed the same wasn't true for Milo.

"Hey, love, guess what just arrived?" She didn't look up. "Meg," I said more sharply.

"Hmm?"

"The birth video is here." I held up the envelope for her to see. "I thought we could have a cuppa and watch it together?"

"You want to watch the birth video? I thought you hated them?"

"No. I'd like to." I poured her a cup of tea, stirring a cube of brown sugar into it, adding a dash of milk, then patted the sofa. "Come and sit with me." She stared at me wordlessly for a moment, then shrugged and climbed off the windowsill, coming to perch on the edge of the sofa cushion. I reached over to Milo, unstrapping him from the bouncy-chair and placing him in Meg's arms. A flash of annoyance crossed her features, but I ignored it. Mum said to keep giving him to her and eventually it would click. It *had to* click.

Her back was poker straight as she waited for me to put the disk in the DVD player. She held Milo with stiff arms, cage like, not at all soft. To anyone who didn't know her, they would think she was some distant aunt who'd had no experience with babies and would rather keep it that way. I looked back to the DVD player as the disk finally loaded, pressed play and went to sit back down next to Megan. She offered me the baby instantly, but I shook my head, picking up my tea. "I don't want to spill on him, you just relax, he's happy with you."

She stared at me, and the look in her eyes was one that caused my stomach to twist. I couldn't remember ever seeing her look at me like that before. Like she hated me for making her hold her own child. The music on the television kicked in and finally she looked away from me, focusing on the screen. The film was tastefully done, just as Toby's had been.

There were lots of black and white stills inserted with soft music over the top. An image of me holding a stack of folded towels, laughing at something someone has said. The midwife massaging Megan's lower back as she rested her elbows on the kitchen counter. The two of us leaned into one another, our foreheads touching as she kneeled in the birth-pool.

The images switched to film and the camera zoomed in on Megan and I from across the room. I had been so wrapped up in Megan and what I could do to make things easier for her, that I'd barely registered the presence of the camera. It meant we'd been caught in our most natural states. No false smiles or awkward quips, just us, as we were. As we'd always been.

I watched the film intently, my hands wrapping tighter around my teacup as the version of me from nine days ago leaned in, whispering something into her ear between contractions. She threw her head back, laughing, eyes sparkling and all at once I was hit with an absolute feeling of despair and desolation. It was like watching a completely different person. That woman, the laughing, beautiful, alive woman, radiant even in the throws of labour, was *my* wife. The woman I'd fallen in love with in the mountains of Nepal. Sure, we'd had our rough patches, our fights and fall outs, but never in all the time I'd known her had she been so out of reach.

This person sitting beside me now, was like a stranger. I no longer knew how to bring her back to me. What to say to make things better. I couldn't remember the last time I'd seen her smile, let alone laugh. Certainly not since Milo had been four or five days old. She was a robot. A shell of a person, the things that made her who she was scraped out and left to rot, leaving nothing of herself behind. And I missed her. I missed the real Megan. I wanted her back, but I had no idea where she'd gone, or how to go about fixing this.

The music began to fade away, replaced by the rolling moans and grunts that signified the end was near. I watched the fear in my own eyes as the Megan on screen went into herself, summoning her strength, needing space to reach the finish line. Her scream was primal, raw and disturbing. Every hair on my arms and the back of my neck raised as I relived the whole experience. She gripped the sides of the birth pool, moving into a squat, and with one echoing shriek that seemed to go on forever, coming from the depths of her soul, the baby was born, his eyes open beneath the cloudy water of the pool. Megan, shaking and flushed from her exertions, reached down with both hands.

Instinctively, I moved to support her, to stop her from falling, cradling her back as she scooped our baby into her arms, looking down at his face with an expression of wonder and awe. "Hello, little one," she whispered. "I've been waiting for you."

Tears filled my eyes and I turned towards Megan on the sofa. Her face was questioning as she watched herself lift the tiny baby to her face, kissing his eyes, one after the other, then his cheeks, and finally his tiny pink lips. She looked away from the television, down to the baby in her arms, then finally, her eyes met mine. "I wish we'd got to keep that one. He was so cute. I really think it would have been the better choice."

I gave a half smile, trying to work out the joke. "What do you mean?" I asked finally.

"I wonder where he went. I remember him. Do you know?" She stared at me with blank, unfocused eyes.

"I don't like this game, Meg. Stop pissing around. That's Milo, right there in your arms. You do know that, right?"

She looked down. "I wish you could see," she said sadly. She handed him to me and moved to the television, crouching down, her fingers touching the screen, running over the smile on her own lips, the tuft of dark hair on Milo's head. I couldn't watch. I could not cope with her nonsense any more. I stood up, leaving the room, taking my son with me.

Chapter Nine

Megan

I didn't know how long I'd been crouching in front of the television, my fingertips running over the paused screen, thinking of the baby I'd hoped for, mourning the fact that he'd gone and I'd been left with an imposter, but it was long enough for my legs to seize up, cramp running down the backs of my calves demanding movement with a flurry of spasms.

Still, I had stayed there, ignoring the burning pain in my muscles, staring at the image of my own face, the sparkle in my eyes, even through the haze of exhaustion post labour. I *had* been happy. In that moment I'd felt like I would burst with the joy of it all.

Where had that feeling gone to? Why couldn't I seem to get it back? It was almost as if I was looking at someone else, someone who looked like me, but who I could neither understand nor relate to. I could have watched that screen all day. It was the sound of Toby waking from his nap that finally broke the spell, his cry echoing down the stairs then stopping almost immediately.

I stood, shaking the life back into my deadened limbs, wincing as the blood rushed back into them, then hobbled as quickly as I could manage up to his room, finding Nate already there. He was sitting on the edge of Toby's bed, one arm around his shoulders, the other cradling Milo. Toby, with his fluffy bed-head and the rosy red cheeks he always had after a long nap, stretched his arms up to me in a wordless request as I entered, and I reached down to pick him up, bringing him to my chest, sniffing his hair, holding him as tight as I could without hurting him. *God, I loved this child. I loved him so much I could actually burst.*

He snuggled into my neck and I waited, knowing it wouldn't last for long. Sure enough, moments later and full of beans once again, he wriggled out of my arms and ran out of the room, babbling something about finding his blue train, the one Grandma had bought him. I made to follow but Nate called me back. "Wait, Megan. We need to talk."

I paused in the doorway, only half listening, my body willing me to follow my child. "Talk about what?"

"You." I glanced at him and saw how serious his expression was. He pursed his lips, his free hand tapping his knee in the way he always did when he was annoyed with me. *Wonderful.* Just what I needed right now, a pointless argument. "Look," he said, taking a deep breath, his nostrils flaring. "I know it's a big change, and I know you've been tired, recovering from giving birth and all that, but this can't continue. I'm sorry to have to say it, but you need to make more effort."

His words were like a red flag to a bull. I was in no mood for being accused of laziness, not when I could count the hours of sleep I'd had over the past week on one hand. "Are you joking, Nate? All I bloody do is try to get it right. Try and make a nice home for you, to make your life easier. You have seen how clean this house is, right? I was up all night cleaning up. Making sure Toby was okay while *you* slept. And you tell me I need to do more? I'm not bloody superwoman!"

"No, that's not what I'm saying. Not at all. I *know* you've been rushing round like a mad thing, and I know you're not sleeping, but you're doing the stuff *I* could be doing. Or Mum if you would let her, she's desperate to help," he sighed. "What I'm saying, is that you're not doing the things you're really needed for."

He looked down at Milo, then back to me, his voice softening now. "You're rejecting him because you're afraid to make Toby jealous. I *know* you are, Meg. I can't figure out how much of this is about Toby and how much is about him being a boy, when we both know how much you wanted a girl, but to be quite honest, I don't care anymore, because whatever the reason, this needs to end. You're being selfish, denying this poor baby his chance to bond with you. *You* are the one who always talks about how important this stage is, how much they're learning and developing and the importance of holding them close, doing skin-to-skin, breastfeeding them. I don't understand what this is, this weird distance you've created between yourself and Milo, but you need to pull yourself together."

"Pull myself together? As if it's that simple."

"You aren't trying. You're hiding away, Meg. Apart from that horrible trip to Ikea, you haven't even left the house since Milo was born. And it's not as if you've been in bed bonding with the baby. *That* I could understand. You did it with Toby and I know how important it was to both of you. But this is different. You need to get outside, get back to normal."

"I can't, Nate. It's not safe out there."

"What? See this is *exactly* what I'm talking about. You're getting overly dramatic. Building things up in your head. You need to snap out of this and step up. Your family needs you, for goodness sake. *I* need you. You've pretty much abandoned me to do it all by myself and this is *not* what I signed up for."

"You aren't being fair," I said, walking over to the window, throwing the curtains back noisily. I stared out of the window, watching the cars move up and down the road outside, the gulls chasing each other across the crisp blue sky. It looked like a summers day out there, but I knew if I opened the window, I would be rewarded with a blast of icy cold air. Autumn was coming to an end, and it felt like the endless dark evenings and cold days would last forever.

I turned around, numbness spreading through me, at a loss at how I could possibly explain what was going on inside my mind. It was impossible to justify my behaviour, I knew it. And for the first time, I realised the problem may not be the baby. It might actually be me. And that was even more frightening. How did you win a battle against yourself?

Nate was standing, facing me, his arms empty. "Neither are you," he said quietly.

I glanced around, searching for Milo and saw him prone on his back on a play-mat in the middle of the floor between us. For a second, time seemed to freeze, images flashing brightly across my mind, a living nightmare playing out in my head. I snapped my head up, shaking with fear and rage, my stomach churning. "What on earth do you think you are doing? Pick him up! Pick him up now, you can't just leave him in the middle of the fucking floor!"

Nate blinked, looking at me like I was completely mad. He didn't move. I rushed forward, grabbing the baby roughly, thrusting him into Nate's chest. "You can't do that! You can't!" I shouted. "Don't you know not to put a baby on the floor like that? It isn't safe!"

Nate stared at me. "I'm surprised you even care," he said, his mouth set in a hard line. "You know you're acting like a fucking lunatic, right?" I stared at him, open mouthed, as he left the room without waiting for an answer.

"I know," I whispered to the empty room. He was right. I was losing my mind. It was the only logical explanation. Babies were not born evil. They just weren't. I was losing myself. Struggling to figure out where the boundary lay between what was normal, rational behaviour and what was not. The line between reality and delusion. But when I'd seen Milo on the floor, just a couple of steps from where I stood, I'd suddenly been consumed by an overwhelming, all encompassing urge to stamp on his tiny, fragile face, and wipe him out for good. And even *I* didn't need to be told that there was something horribly wrong about that.

Chapter Ten

Jane

I opened Nate's kitchen cupboard, pulling out a tin of loose tea and the floral pot I'd bought as a housewarming gift, way back before Megan had moved in with him. Spooning the tea leaves into the pot and listening to the sounds of Megan clattering about in the bedroom above me, I reflected back to the first time I'd met her.

Nate had had plenty of girlfriends in the past, but Megan was the first one that had made me feel worried. She was so different from the others, and the way Nate looked at her made me nervous. She wasn't the type of woman I would have chosen for my son, I would have preferred a sweet, quiet girl, not this headstrong woman with an obvious wild side. Of course, I had seen instantly why Nate was so fascinated by her. There was no denying that she was beautiful and vivacious, and she carried with her an air of freedom that was intoxicating. But I'd expected – hoped – that their fling would burn bright and fast, coming to an end sooner rather than later. To my surprise, it hadn't worked that way. Instead of flitting off to her next adventure, she had stayed.

Nate had moved out of the home we'd shared together when he was twenty-seven years old, having worked hard and saved harder for the deposit to buy his own place. I knew he felt guilty about leaving me, and my instinct had been to beg and cry, to insist he stay with me forever. The idea of waking up to a big empty house and coming home to the same, filled me with sadness. I wasn't sure he knew how intensely I needed him, how much my world revolved around meeting his needs.

Other than my part time job at the garden centre, I had nothing but my son. I'd wanted to cause a scene and talk him out of his plans. But I hadn't. I'd kept my mouth closed, knowing that the more I pulled him closer, the more desperately he would try to run. For my silence, I was rewarded.

Nate was such a good boy. I should have known he would never abandon me completely. He wanted his own space, his own life as a man, but he didn't let me down. He bought a large fixer upper, just two roads from my own house, and when he took me on the five minute walk to see it for the first time, I couldn't hold back the tears. I should have known he wouldn't abandon me completely.

For a while, I was happy. He never seemed to mind me turning up unannounced, in fact, he was grateful when I stopped by to cook him his favourite dinners and run the hoover round. He never did enjoy the domestic side of home ownership. But when he arrived home from Nepal with this firecracker of a girl, and she continued to stay with him week after week, month after month, I was scared. I wondered if this time, he really *would* leave me. If she would take him back to Kent with her eventually, or worse, to join her parents in Australia after they'd emigrated.

My son, flying off to the other side of the world. He was an adventurous boy. He would *love* it. The fear had consumed me for months, years even as I'd waited to hear their plans for the future, never daring to ask, to appear pushy. I'd already made up my mind that wherever they went, whatever difficulties it might present, I would go too. I would follow my boy to the ends of the earth.

In the end, though, I didn't have to. It had been Megan who declared they would stay in the house Nate had bought for himself. She had fallen in love with Brighton and she adored the bright, warm house Nate had renovated with care and attention. They would stay. For good. That was the moment in which I stopped thinking of her as a competitor, and started to feel some warmth for the girl. She could have destroyed my world in the blink of an eye, but she hadn't, and I was grateful to her for that.

I carried the tea tray into the living room. Toby was in bed for the night, and Milo was sound asleep in Nate's arms, Nate's head lolling back against the cushions, his eyes only half open. I put the tray down on the table. "Give him to me," I instructed. "You pour."

He shook himself awake, blinking. "Oh, yeah, sorry," he apologised, struggling to sit up.

"You need to be careful, darling. You could drop him if you fall asleep like that. It isn't safe."

"I know. I know, I didn't mean to. I'm just so tired." He passed Milo into my outstretched arms and I smiled as his warm, compact body nestled against me. It made my heart swell to have a newborn in the family again. There was nothing quite so special as these first few months, where every single thing was a wondrous miracle in their fresh, inquisitive minds. Nate rubbed his eyes and picked up the pot of tea, pouring a generous cup for both of us. A third remained empty.

"Won't she come down?" I asked, gesturing to the ceiling.

"I don't think so."

"What's she even doing up there? She isn't sleeping, I could hear her banging around like a heard of wildebeest from the kitchen. It's enough to wake poor Toby."

Nate shook his head. "He's a heavy sleeper. He'll be fine."

"But, *why* is she staying up there? Leaving you to see to Milo?" *Again,* I added silently. It hadn't escaped my attention that Megan was not as hands on with

Milo as she'd always been with Toby, and it gave me an uneasy feeling in the pit of my stomach.

Nate shrugged. "I don't know, Mum. I don't know what's got into her lately. She's not quite back to normal yet. I guess it's her hormones."

I looked up sharply. "Do you think she's ill?"

"Ill?"

"Yes, *ill*, Nate. *Unwell*. In her mind, I mean?"

He pursed his lips and I rocked Milo back and forth, waiting for his response. "No," he said finally. "No, I don't. I think she's sad because of Toby."

"What do you mean?"

He sighed. "He's still so small, and you know how close the two of them are. I think she's realising it will never be just the two of them again. Things have changed, and she's mourning what she feels she's lost. That's what I think it is."

"But look at what she's gained," I exclaimed, though I could see his answer made sense. Watching Megan and Toby had been something I could soak up for hours. They reminded me of how Nate and I had been when he was tiny like that. So close, so very in tune with each other. I could understand her feeling guilt over adding a new person into the mix. "It's not fair on Milo, though," I said softly. "She chose to bring him into this world. It's no good overthinking it now. It's done."

"I know that."

"But does she? Have you spoken to her about it?"

He nodded. "Yes. But you know how she can be. She's headstrong."

"Then you're going to have to push her. You make it too easy for her to absent herself, Nate. You do a lot more than most men would." I looked away suddenly, hoping my words hadn't made him think about his own absent father, the fact that he hadn't even stayed to be a part of his sons life, let alone been the kind of dad Nate had become.

I took a long drink of my tea, then placed the cup down beside me. "What I mean is, perhaps by doing so much, you're making it take longer for her to bond with him. She needs time alone with *both* of them to see that it's okay. That she has more than enough love for them both."

He looked at me, considering my words and I got the distinct impression that there was something he wasn't telling me. "Nate, you are sure she's not unwell?" I asked again. "It can happen, after a baby is born."

"I mean, maybe it's a case of the baby-blues or something, but I would know if it were something more than that," he said. "I know her better than anyone."

I nodded. That was true, he did. And he was the type of man who would pick up on little changes. I was sure of it. He was a decent, caring man, and I knew he'd be the first to say if he thought there was something wrong with Megan. "Okay," I smiled, relieved at his answer. "Then you need to push her. Be cruel to be kind. She'll get there, darling. How could she not fall for this little sweetheart?" I grinned, squeezing the tiny bundle in my arms.

Chapter Eleven

Megan

"Nate." I was standing in the kitchen doorway, watching as my husband dashed from one side of the room to the other, picking up dirty cups and bowls, dropping them into the bowl of steaming, soapy water, turning off the tap, flicking the switch on the kettle. He leaned over the hob, stirring the soup simmering in a pan, then bent down, throwing a wet tea-towel into the washing machine.

He looked angry. And exhausted. We hadn't spoken a word to one another since the argument in Toby's room yesterday, but I knew I couldn't put this conversation off any longer. I'd been up all night trying to figure out what to do, pacing relentlessly back and forth beside Toby's bed. My legs aches with the exertion of it, but even now, I couldn't stay still. I was nervous. Fidgety. I still wasn't sure how to even begin to make Nate understand what I needed to tell him, but I knew for certain that I wasn't ready to look after the boys alone. I simply wasn't capable. And honestly, I didn't know if I could be sure to keep Milo safe. *From myself.* I felt sick having admitted the truth to myself in the wee hours of this morning, but it gave me the courage to ask for help.

"Nate," I said again, my voice louder this time.

"What, Megan?" he said, his voice cold. He continued to dart around, not pausing to look me in the eye.

"I – I need to talk to you."

"Go ahead."

"I, well... maybe we can sit down for a minute?"

"I'm kinda busy here, can you just spit it out."

"Nate!"

He turned to me, one hand scraping roughly through his hair. It was greasy and limp, and he hadn't shaved. His burgundy woollen jumper had a pull in the front of it, and his mouth was set in a firm, straight line. "Look, Meg. I've got a thousand things to do and I doubt it will be more than a couple of minutes before one of the boys needs me, and since *you* seem to have checked out of all your mothering responsibilities, it's all on my fucking shoulders. So forgive me if I don't have time for a little chat right now."

I stared at him, gob-smacked. I couldn't remember a time when he'd ever spoken to me like that, or looked at me with such malice. If I hadn't been building up to this talk for the past twelve hours, I would have walked out and slammed the door behind me, but I knew what I had to say couldn't wait. "Fine," I said, clasping my hands in front of me, trying in vain to keep them still. "I'll just say it then. I don't want you to go back to work." The words came out in a rush, and I waited in silence for his response.

His mouth opened and closed. He rubbed his temples in fast circles as if he could make sense of what I'd said. Finally, he spoke. "What are you talking about?"

"You're due back after the weekend. It's too soon. I want you to call them and tell them you aren't coming."

"Why on earth would I do that?"

I took a deep breath, gripping hold of the doorframe for support. "I think it's obvious, Nate. Don't you?" I sighed. "I'm not coping. Not even with you here. I'm struggling, Nate. I haven't slept, not in days. I can barely take care of myself."

I looked down at the floor, ashamed at what I had to say, yet knowing I had no choice. "I *can't* do this. You know I can't." I couldn't bring myself to say what I really meant. That I knew I wasn't capable of looking after the baby, that I couldn't be his mother. That I was seeing things I knew nobody else could see, feeling things that terrified me, and that I was sure I was losing my mind. What I wanted to scream at the top of my lungs was, *I can't cope with him, please don't leave me alone with him. I'm scared of what will happen.*

Instead, I stepped forward, holding his stare despite the fact that I wanted to run upstairs to my room and hide from the reality of my situation. "Something isn't right. I know it isn't. It's not normal, Nate. I can't seem to slow down. I can't keep track of my thoughts. If I lie down, I feel like I'm suffocating. I need to be up, moving, all the time. I'm barely able to swallow a mouthful of food without feeling like I'm choking. You can't be oblivious to this, Nate. You *know* this isn't how things should be. It's been almost two weeks since that baby arrived, and every day it gets more and more difficult. I can't do this without you, I need you to stay home. Don't leave me on my own, Nate. Please. Please don't go back." I heard the desperation in my own voice. All I wanted was for him to step forward and take me in his arms and hold me tight. To tell me he knew what was wrong and he could fix this. He could make it better. I wanted him to promise he wouldn't leave me to deal with everything by myself.

Instead, he looked me in the eye and shook his head and I felt the world ripped out from under me in one sharp tug. "I can't not go back, Megan. You're being unfair to even ask. How would we pay the bills? Put food on the table? They were bloody good to give me two weeks full pay for paternity leave in the first place, you said it yourself."

He stepped forward, pulling me into his chest, hugging me tightly, but it wasn't the hug I'd needed. It was all wrong. An apology rather than a promise. A goodbye wrapped up in sugar coated words of rejection.

"I know it's difficult," he said. "Believe me, I do know. But it's probably just the baby blues or something like that, sweetheart. Everything has changed, and I get that you feel guilty about Toby being pushed out, but you're taking it way too far in your desperation to over-compensate. You're pushing Milo out instead, and the poor little guy needs you so much more than Toby does right now. Don't you remember how it was with Toby? You were his everything. All he wanted for that first year. Milk and mummy cuddles and nothing else would do. And Milo needs you just the same. He's really missed out."

I stayed silent, breathing hard, pushing my face against the wool of his sweater as tears sprang to my eyes, stinging as I tried to fight them. He continued to talk, his voice rumbling deeply in his chest, the sounds echoing against my ear. "Your hormones are wild and you're not sleeping. Of course you're struggling, love. I am too." He stroked my hair and I kept my face pressed into his chest. "Look," he said. "I'll tell you what. I'm going to give the doctor's surgery a ring now and book you in to be seen. I'm sure they'll say it's nothing, but if it will help you feel more confident when you're on your own, we should give it a go. I should be able to get you in as an emergency for this evening. Get this dealt with before I go back on Monday. You can go and have a good chat with Doctor Barnard and tell her how you're feeling and maybe get something to help you feel calmer. Loads of mums need something to take the edge off in the first few months, don't they? It's nothing to be ashamed of."

"You mean, something like anti-depressants?" I said, pulling back abruptly.

"Yeah, why not?"

"I'm not depressed."

"No. But like you said, you're not yourself. I'm sure they can figure out what to do. Will you go, if I sort the appointment?"

I shrugged. Talking to the doctor was the last thing I wanted to do, but I knew things couldn't go on the way they were. I *did* need help. I nodded slowly. "I suppose so."

"Good." He kissed the top of my head and turned back to the soup now boiling over in the pan. "We'll get through this, Megan. Sometimes, you just have to face things head on and it becomes easier. You just need to get back in the game."

Chapter Twelve

Megan

The waiting room was surprisingly busy for quarter to six in the evening. I'd assumed, mistakenly that most people would be gone for the day. I'd hoped it would be quiet. Instead, Nate had dropped me off outside and I'd come in to discover the doctor was running an hour behind schedule. An hour to sit quietly and act like it was all okay.

I could feel so many eyes on me, watching me, making judgements. I got up from my seat, walking to the notice board, looking but not seeing, pretending, like always. I glanced behind me, seeing the blank faces of the patients as they followed me with their eyes. Did they know I'd left my children with their father so I could be here? Could they tell that I was simultaneously relieved at being out from under the same roof as my newborn, yet consumed with blind terror about the safety of my toddler? Could they see the conflict spinning out of control inside my head?

I wiped my sweat-coated palms against my jogging

bottoms for the hundredth time, walking over to a different seat, then standing up almost instantly to pace over to the window. Now that I was here, I wasn't so sure it was a good idea.

Professionals – doctors, nurses, social workers, teachers, the police even, they were all supposed to help you. To make life safer. Better. But I knew that it didn't always work that way. Sometimes the people you were supposed to trust were the ones you needed to be afraid of. If I walked into Doctor Barnard's room and told her the real facts of what was happening in my head, all my fears, completely unfiltered, the pure, horrific truth of what was happening in my mind, she might decide that I was a danger to my children. She might take them from me. She might take Toby.

And if she did that, not only would I not be able to keep him safe from Milo, but I had no way of knowing what else Milo may do out of my sight. Who else he might hurt. I had to keep them with me. Close. At home. I couldn't risk losing my children.

I wiped my palms against my trousers again and

then raked them through my unbrushed nest of hair. Making up my mind, I turned briskly for the exit, walking fast. I was almost at the door when a buzzer sounded loudly and a raspy voice came over the Tannoy. "Mrs M. Taylor to room four please."

"That's you, love," the receptionist called to me, nodding in the direction of the hallway that led to the Doctors rooms. I paused, moving from one foot to another, indecision flooding my mind. "Well, go on then," she said, smiling warmly.

I gave a slow nod. "Okay," I whispered. I walked past her, feeling the heat of her stare burn into my back, along with that of everyone else. The corridor was dimly lit and quiet as I made my way down it. The door to room four was slightly ajar and I pushed it open slowly, not moving from the doorway.

Doctor Barnard had been my GP ever since I moved from Kent to Brighton to live with Nate. She was hard to read and could be brusk if she felt you were wasting her time, not like the kindly old family GP I'd had back in Ashford. The sweet old Doctor Northney. He had been easy to talk to. He never made you feel like you had to hurry to explain yourself so he could get on with his day.

Doctor Barnard was probably far more suited to the new ways of the ever stretched NHS with her efficiency, but because I hated to feel I'd taken one of her precious appointments, it meant I often didn't bother to come, even when I probably should have. I'd spent enough time during my school years being sent out in the corridor for saying the wrong thing, or reprimanded in front of my peers. I didn't appreciate being sent home with my tail between my legs as an adult.

"Mrs Taylor. Take a seat," she said, pointing to the chair beside her desk. I stepped into the room, pushing the door closed behind me, hyper aware that I had to be careful with my words, but that I wouldn't be here unless I really did need her help. I had to find a way of letting her know just how much I was struggling, yet not let on about my feelings towards Milo. Even I knew that it wasn't okay to think the thoughts I'd had about him. Mothers didn't dislike their babies. Good mothers didn't find their skin crawling with the urge to throw their children when they were forced to hold and feed them. The room smelt strongly of coffee, and as I sat down, the doctor picked up a chipped mug and downed its contents in one go. Her eyes were heavy and she looked like she was ready for her working week to be done. I was sure her mind was already half focused on a takeaway and some mindless Friday night television.

"So," she said, tapping her pencil on her desk. "How can I help you today? I see you've come without baby. Is there an issue with your stitches?"

"No." I'd had four after the birth, a small tear which thankfully was healing well. I paused, looking at my feet, tapping the tips of my fingers against my thumbs in a rapid motion. I clasped my hands together and held them tightly between my knees to stop them from fidgeting. "I... I'm not feeling myself... I'm not coping... as well as I'd like," I added quickly, already afraid that I'd said too much. "I haven't been sleeping."

She frowned. "I see. A new mum who isn't

sleeping. That's pretty much par for the course, I'm afraid. Babies tend not to let their mummies sleep."

"No, that's not quite what I mean. He's sleeping. I'm not."

"Right." She rubbed her left temple with two fingers, pursing her mouth. "Is your husband still on paternity?"

"He goes back Monday."

"Then I suggest you use this weekend to have a few afternoon naps and get your sleep back on track. What about your moods? Are you crying a lot?"

"I..." I shook my head. I hadn't cried, hardly at all. I didn't feel sad... I felt angry and scared and frantic, like something terrible was about to happen and only I seemed to be aware of it. Like I was standing on the edge of the shore, watching as an enormous tsunami rolled at breakneck speed towards me, its shadow casting darkness over everything in its path, yet everyone around me was sunbathing and eating ice-cream. Pulling their children closer to paddle and dig in the sticky, wet sand, unaware that they were about to be swept up. Ignorant to the fact that everything was about to change. "No," I answered finally. "I haven't been crying. But I haven't felt like myself. My thoughts are... jumbled... I'm," I paused, trying to think of the right word. "Fearful."

"That's normal. It's all completely to be expected. You're a mum to two now, Megan. You can expect many years of jumbled thoughts and fears for their futures. It's a scary world out there, but I've no doubt you'll bring them through it. Now," she said, leaning back. "I suspect this is a classic case of baby blues. I seem to remember you got off lightly with your firstborn, so perhaps that's why you're noticing it more this time. But it's common. In fact, you're the ninth mother I've seen this week going through this exact thing. And I'll tell you what I told all of them. Get outside. Go for walks with your baby and make sure you're getting a good hour – at the very least – of fresh air and exercise each day. On top of that, try a warm bath before bed and some chamomile tea. And when you get up to feed in the night, make sure you keep the lights low so you don't rouse yourself too much and can get back to sleep quickly afterwards. All this should pass in a week or so, but parenting a newborn isn't easy. The first years are the hardest."

I stared at her. "I don't think it's the baby blues. I really think it's worse than that."

She gave a condescending smile. "Everyone thinks they have it worse. Believe me, you're fine. You just need to get out of the house and pick up your routines again. If you're no better in a week, come back and we'll talk again. But for now, I still have three more patients to see and you have children to be getting back to." She waited, pointedly, lips pursed, as I rose to my feet and walked out, shutting the door behind me. I wished I hadn't bothered to come.

Chapter Thirteen

Megan

"So you never said how it went," Nate said, lowering Milo into the Moses basket on my side of the bed and walking around to his side. He yanked off his clothes, throwing them on the chair beside the dressing table, then climbed between the sheets, his leg touching mine. I fought the urge to get up. I had to try and sleep tonight. The doctor had been an absolute bitch, but still, she was right that sleep would make things better. It would give me perspective.

I fidgeted, pulling my leg out from under his and propping my pillows up on the headboard, leaning back against them with a heavy sigh. "She thinks it's lack of routine combined with baby blues," I shrugged. My eyes pleaded with him to disagree. I wanted him to push the issue. To tell me to go back and demand they take me more seriously. I knew she was wrong.

"That's what I thought. Mum agrees too, I think. You need to get your normal habits back on track, that's all." I stayed silent, staring at a point on the opposite wall. "Did she tell you to come back in?" he asked, taking off his watch and dropping it on the bedside table.

"In a week. If nothing changes." It felt like a lifetime away. It was hard enough getting through each minute.

"I'm sure it will. Couple of days and you'll be back to the Megan we remember. I bet it will be easier when I'm back at work. You'll have the space to do your own thing, like you're used to, without me getting in your way." He kissed me briefly, then turned on his side, his back towards me, his arm stretching out to flick the switch on the bedside lamp, casting the room into darkness. "Night, darling, try to get some sleep."

"Goodnight." I sat in the dark, gently rocking back and forth, trying to contain my pent-up energy, to will my body into relaxation. Waiting for Nate to fall asleep was torturous. When, eventually, I heard his breathing grow slower and heavier, I slipped out of bed, past the Moses basket and out of the bedroom.

I'd put on my nightdress, determined to make an effort to create a decent bedtime routine for myself, but it was no good. I wouldn't sleep. I could feel the energy fizzing in my veins, the need to run, move, escape.

Quietly, I went down the stairs, unlocked the front door and walked out into the darkness, leaving the door wide open in my wake. I shivered, but I didn't slow as I walked determinedly along the quiet street, heading towards the narrow lanes, following the familiar route down to the beach. Most of the shops were closed, but there were still plenty of people moving in and out of restaurants, heading in riotous crowds towards the bass heavy music coming from the pub. A homeless woman called to me from a doorway, asking for money I clearly didn't have, and I shivered harder, realising with a strange kind of numbness that I was very, very cold. I'd left without a coat or shoes, but it was too late to think about that now. I couldn't go back.

I turned onto Black Lion Street, the moon high and bright above me as I walked barefoot along the filthy pavement, past more crowded pubs, warm looking restaurants closing up for the night. A group of four men on the pavement ahead of me stopped to stare as I approached. "Nice nightie!" one shouted, laughing as if he'd cracked the best joke in the history of comedy.

"I can see her nips!" another chimed in. "They're fucking enormous. Like udders!"

"Oy love, come here, I'll warm you up," a third shouted, jabbing his friend in the ribs with his elbow, a physical plea for acceptance from the group. Like primates displaying their arses to show how macho they were. Their words meant nothing to me. It was as if they were on a TV soap and I was only watching from a safe distance. I kept walking in a straight line, passing right by them without so much as turning my head. Their catcalls followed, echoing behind me, but they stayed put. I felt no sense of relief.

I crossed the road, the beach finally in my sights as I made my way down the sloping path, glad to find myself alone for a moment. I stepped off the pavement onto the shingle and hesitated, gasping at the pain of the pebbles digging into the soles of my freezing feet. It was almost unbearable. *Almost.* But I couldn't stop now. I had to get to the sea, where I could wash away the layers of dirt that clouded my vision, distorting my thoughts. The seawater would cleanse me, make me see everything clearly again.

I was sure I was right. *This* was what I needed to do to be a good mother, to prove my strength and show how much I was willing to put myself through for the sake of my children. I was prepared to try anything now. Anything to make these terrifying thoughts disappear.

I stumbled, wincing and hissing over the sharp stones, stopping every few steps, gathering my resolve, surging forward again, until I reached the deep midnight blue ocean. The wind whipped against me, sending freezing sprays of seawater into my face, my eyes watering as I took my first determined step into the frigid water.

The pain was enough to make me stop, flames and blades of ice attacking my feet, my calves. I forced myself to move again, biting down on the inside my my cheek as the pain spread up my thighs, around my waist. I gritted my teeth, stared up at the moon and then back to the inky water rushing around my body. I was alone. More alone than I'd ever been in my life. I felt like it didn't matter what I said or did now. Nobody would hear me. Nobody would take me seriously until it was too late. Until something had happened that could never be undone. Only *I* could fix this now. And if it hurt, all the better. I probably deserved it.

I sucked in a deep breath and with my eyes wide open, I dived forward, throwing myself beneath the bitterly cold surface.

Chapter Fourteen

Megan

The shaking had lasted for hours. At one point, I'd been convinced I would never warm up, sure that I'd pushed my body too hard, past the brink of no return. That gradually, the sensation of ice pouring through my veins would become less and less painful, until eventually I would slip into unconsciousness and fade peacefully away. It would be so easy. A silent goodbye. And perhaps in the end, it would be better for everyone if I simply went to sleep and never woke up. They wouldn't realise it, but it would be a kindness.

Walking home from the beach had been so much more agonising than the journey there. My memories of coming back home were blurred, colours and lights and voices playing in broken snippets, my thoughts confused and random. Somehow, I had made it back, surprised to find the door standing wide open, the house mercifully quiet. I'd stumbled into the living room, turned the gas fire on to max and wrapped myself in every coat I could find from the cupboard under the stairs.

I'd been scared then. Waiting for the shock to kick in and finish me off, to stop my heart and cloak me in inescapable darkness, yet for some reason it never came. Eventually, I'd felt able to climb out from beneath the pile of coats, and unfold myself from the nest I'd created on the carpet. I'd needed to see. To know if my efforts had been in vain.

Slowly, with a mingled sense of trepidation and excitement, I'd climbed the stairs, popping my head in to Toby's room to check on him, then going to my bedroom where Nate still slept soundly. I'd leaned over the Moses basket, lifting Milo into my arms, carrying him out before he could make a sound.

I think I knew immediately. I just couldn't bring myself to admit it. I went back downstairs, turning the fire down to one bar, before sitting curled up in the corner of the sofa. His eyes were still closed, but his mouth rooted, and I unbuttoned my nightdress, now dry, but crispy with seawater, and brought his mouth to my nipple, letting him feed. I watched his face, his mouth, the tiny flickers of his eyelids, the clench and release of his tiny fists against my bare skin. When he had finished, I laid him along my thighs, his head propped up on my knees, his feet pointed towards my stomach, and covered him with his blanket. I willed myself to love him. To want to protect him. To squash down the fear that bubbled within me as I looked at him now. Because nothing had changed. Not even a little bit.

I'd been so sure, so very sure that it would work. I'd put myself through the pain of the icy cold water, because I had believed it would cleanse me of this hatred I held for my own son. *My son*. Even that didn't draw a response from me, except to think of Toby.

This child was worse than a stranger to me. I'd never experienced such powerful feelings of such negative depths for any person in my whole life. Not even the girls who'd pressed chewing gum into my hair in year nine, and hidden cigarettes in my bag before reporting me to Mr. Marshall, the head teacher, had elicited such a bone-deep loathing in response.

I had no clue what to do now, but I knew one thing. I could not keep pretending. Hoping it would somehow fix itself. But Nate had brushed off my worries, and even my doctor had told me to pull myself together. I didn't know who else to turn to. Certainly not Jane, who would love nothing more than the opportunity to take over and steal my children out from under me. There was nobody I could trust. I was alone in this, and I had run out of ideas.

I watched Milo's face, feeling lost and confused, the heat of the room stifling now, my eyes growing heavy, though I fought to keep them open. I let my head lean back against the sofa, blinking fast, trying to stay awake, still watching him beneath heavy eyelids. The heat was so intense. I knew I should get up to turn the fire off, but I couldn't will myself to move. I was tired. So very tired. It had been so long since I'd last closed my eyes. Days, in fact. If I just shut them, just for a moment, that would be enough. Just a little rest...

"I will kill Toby. And you too."

I gasped, thrust into consciousness, my heart thrumming hard in my chest, my eyes wide open now, staring down at the baby in my lap. He was awake, looking up at me with black, hate filled eyes. "What did you say?" I asked, my voice barely a whisper.

"I said, I'm glad I found you. I was wondering where you two had disappeared off to," Nate replied from the living room doorway. I shook my head, looking towards the sound of his voice, blinking as I tried to focus on his face.

"Did... did you say something else? Just a second ago?"

"Nope. Christ almighty, it's hot in here. I know winter's on the way, but you may have gone a bit overboard with the heating, love." He walked over to the fire, turning it off and I looked back down at Milo. *Was it you? It was, wasn't it?* I thought, staring into his eyes, trying to communicate silently. I knew he could understand me. He blinked.

"It's so good to see you two spending some time together," Nate said, turning to me with a wide smile.

"I take it you had a better night sleep? I didn't hear you get up."

"No... I... the baby... he wanted feeding. I didn't want to wake you," I lied, my eyes still on Milo's.

He leaned forward, kissing my forehead, then sat down beside me, his hand on Milo's belly. "I wouldn't have minded. You know you don't have to get up and come down here just to feed him?"

I nodded, still looking at the baby. "Can... can you hold him. I want to have a shower."

"Yeah, I'll take the little guy. But I want to pop out to the shops in a bit, do the food shop so you don't have that to worry about when I'm back at work."

"You want to go out?"

"You don't have to come. I know you're not up for it just yet. No rush, love. And you seem to be getting better, so I'm happy to take it slow. I'll go. You can stay here and play with the boys."

"By myself?"

"I won't be long."

"No, Nate, I can't. Not yet. Something might happen."

"Like what?" he grinned. "The worst thing that can come your way is sick or poo related, and you're experienced enough to deal with all of that. Besides, it will be good practice for Monday. You'll be alone all day then. Best to do a test run first."

"I already spoke to you about that."

He frowned. "And like I told you, I have to go in. We have bills to pay, and I'm massively behind on my work. You'll be fine. You're good at this, Meg. You *are*. You just need to build up your confidence again. Now, you go and jump in the shower and I'll get Tobes up."

"Please, stop calling him Tobes."

"Fine. Toby. Whatever. Go." He slid his hands beneath Milo, scooping him up, and instantly I felt as if a huge burden had been lifted from my shoulders. I made my way upstairs, feeling disorientated and panicky. I had to figure out a way to stop Nate from leaving me. Maybe I could call his work and get them to give him more time? Or I could hide his car keys before Monday morning? I had to think of something. I had to make him stay.

"Read it, Mama?" Toby asked, dropping his Postman Pat book onto my lap and climbing up on the sofa beside me. I was bouncing nervously on the edge of my seat, my eyes darting from the baby in the bouncy-chair, to the window and back again.

I'd spent as long as I could get away with in the bathroom, the steam of the hot shower enveloping me, creating a protective womb I had no wish to escape, but eventually, the water had run cold and I'd been forced out of its comforting stream. I'd had a sudden burst of hope when I'd remembered we had ordered the shopping to be delivered a few times in the past, and after I'd dressed, I had suggested it to Nate, sure that he would agree it was the easier option. But it hadn't worked. He'd said we couldn't wait, we needed food today, the cupboards were bare. That didn't matter to me. I couldn't remember the last time I'd eaten anyway, but he'd gone, despite all my protests, and now I was sat here alone with Toby and Milo counting down the minutes until he returned.

I took the book, trying to focus on the words, but

they jumped in front of my eyes, the images swirling, merging until they made no sense whatsoever. I rubbed hard at my eye sockets, but still, I couldn't make out the letters. "I can't right now," I finally admitted, patting Toby's head, passing the book back to him. His bottom lip jutted out, wobbling.

"I want you read it me," he said, pushing the book towards me again. The shrill ring of the land-line sounded from the hall and I jumped up.

"Come with me to see who's calling," I said, relieved to have a distraction. He grinned, climbing off the sofa, the book forgotten as he followed me out to the hall and I picked up the phone, crouching down so he could listen. "Hello?"

"It's only me."

"It's Daddy," I whispered.

"Hi Dada!"

"Hi Tobes... I mean, uh, Toby. Are you having fun with your toys?"

"I made a picture!"

"Great, will you show it to me soon?"

Toby nodded in a wordless answer and I

straightened up so I could talk to Nate. "What's up? Why aren't you back?"

"Nothing's up, darling, I just wanted to check if we needed toilet paper? And foil?"

"I don't know."

"Well, can you check?"

"Just buy some. I can't leave the boys alone."

"Meg, just check will you? I don't want to buy it if we don't need it. The place is already overrun with baby stuff. We barely have any space in the cupboards as it is."

"Oh fine. Hold on." I placed the phone down on the hallway shelf and ran into the kitchen, yanking open a drawer. The cardboard tube for the foil was empty, and I yanked it out, turning to check under the sink for toilet paper. Rushing back to the hall, I grabbed the phone. "No to toilet paper, yes to foil."

"Okay. Got it. So how are you getting on?"

His voice sounded strange. "Nate?"

"Yeah? Can you hear me? There's a crackle on the line. I asked how you're getting on?"

I had the strange sensation that I wasn't talking to

my husband. That someone else was imitating him. The voice was similar, but not enough to fool me. Why would he be calling? Unless... I glanced behind me, realising Toby was gone. *Fuck!* I slammed down the phone, and ran breathlessly into the living room. *I knew it!* That man on the phone wanted to get me away from my son, to put him in danger. Milo was responsible for this, of course he was! I was so stupid to fall for his tricks.

Toby was bent over Milo's bouncy chair, his hand on Milo's cheek. The baby was pretending to sleep, but I was sure he was faking. He was far too clever. What if I'd been a few seconds longer? If that imposter on the phone had managed to keep me talking? What would have happened then? It didn't bear thinking about.

"Toby," I screamed, running towards him. "You were supposed to stay with me! I can't keep you safe if you don't stay with me!" I grabbed his shoulder and yanked him back hard. It seemed to happen in slow motion, the shock on his face, the slow tumble, his legs coming out from under him, his temple cracking hard into the corner of the square coffee table, the tiny trickle of blood running down his cheek. He stared at me, wide eyed, fearful. And then he began to scream.

I'd always been a little bit behind the crowd. A late bloomer, my mum called me, though she'd tried to frame it positively. *Such a good girl. No trouble at all.* I'd been quiet all through my junior school years, kept my head down, by no means an excellent student, just anxious to get by without any trouble. I found that if I looked like I was working, that was enough to keep the teachers off my back. I always handed in my homework, usually scraping a B or C grade, but it was good enough. I had no desire to excel, simply to get through each day without drama.

It wasn't until I turned fifteen and woke up with breasts that had seemed to spring from nowhere, and hormones igniting like a cocktail in my blood stream, that I finally broke out of my shell and began to explore the possibilities that life held in store for me. I made new friends, leaving behind Amy, a quiet, lifeless girl I'd met up with twice weekly since year six, to watch soaps over custard creams and mugs of hot chocolate. I'd never been sure if we were friends or if we just kept up our arrangement so we wouldn't feel so alone. But I was done with soaps. No longer willing to watch life happen through the eyes of a made up character. I wanted to experience things for *myself*.

I discovered that if I did my hair and make-up just right, and wore a push up bra, I could get into clubs with the girls I'd met from year eleven and their older sisters. I stopped worrying about getting told off in school and found that suddenly, my name was on every teacher's lips and to my surprise, I was glad to finally have them notice me. It didn't matter that it was to yell at me. I just liked knowing I existed in their thoughts. I wasn't just a wallflower telling them what they wanted to hear anymore.

I wore tight dresses on Friday nights out in town. I drank shots until I threw up, and then did it all over again the next night. I learned to smoke and found I was good at it. It made me feel powerful and grown up. I kissed every boy I fancied and never bothered to ask for their phone numbers. It was all so immediate. So very *in the moment.* Thinking of tomorrow would have ruined it.

After ten months of wild parties, lost underwear and blurred memories, I'd finally burned out and been forced to calm down a bit. I'd been cooped up in my little box, playing the role of good girl for so long that I had needed to go a bit crazy. To break free of the rules and figure out who I really was beneath all the mumbling and blushing. And I had. I'd unleashed a part of me that couldn't be subdued again, but I didn't need to take it to the extreme any longer. I had nothing left to prove. I slowed down on the nights out, I drank less and I was far more selective when it came to liaisons with the opposite sex. But there was one thing I just couldn't seem to give up. Smoking. I loved it. I didn't want to, but I couldn't seem to bring myself to quit.

I loved the feel of my brain springing into action as I took the first few puffs in the morning, the high mixed with shaky nausea if I smoked it too fast. The instant calm when I was anxious or stressed. I loved having something to do with my hands when I was nervous or slipping back into old introverted habits. Smoking made me confident. It made me brave. Sexy. People would come up to ask for a light and somehow by the time we reached the butt, we'd have become best friends. It was integral to the person I'd transformed into, a magic feather that allowed me to spread my wings and fly, a crutch I couldn't bear to let go of.

I'd kept it up, never contemplating quitting, right up to the day I learned I was pregnant with Toby. By then, I'd cut down my intake from fifteen a day to a mere two, knowing that it wasn't fair to inflict my habit on the baby we were trying for. When I had picked up the test from the bathroom sink after the longest ninety second wait of my life and saw the positive result, I was both elated and devastated.

I wanted this baby. More than anything. But to have him, I was going to have to give up something I adored, something which felt like a part of me, because I knew, I could not have both. I'd cried as I threw away the remainder of the pack, my lighters, the pretty ceramic ashtrays. It all had to go. But I'd had no choice. That part of my life was over and I had to let it go so I could step into the next chapter.

The memory of that day, the determination I'd felt knowing I would never pick up a cigarette again, was clear in my mind as I turned the television on now, flicking to some brightly coloured cartoon, flying dogs with high pitched voices racing across the screen. Toby squatted down on a huge floor cushion, his eyes glued to the intoxicating images. I could remember the power of emotion that had flooded me that day, the depth of sacrifice I was willing to make for my unborn child. Quitting smoking, much as I had loved it, was nothing compared to what I would have done for him. I would have cut off my own hand if it was needed to keep him safe.

And now, I'd ruined it all. After swearing to protect him, to do whatever it took to keep him from harm, *I* had been the one to hurt him. Badly. I couldn't stop myself from leaning down to inspect the side of his head again. After I'd cleaned up the blood, I'd found a small cut, around an inch long, and not very deep, a purple bruise already blooming across his pale skin, spreading out from the edges of the incision. It could have been so much worse. I could have really hurt him. *I could have killed him.* In that moment, anything had been possible. I'd been so lost. So very angry.

I stood up, leaving him in front of the television. I walked to the hallway where Milo was sleeping in his pram and glancing nervously over my shoulder, I strode past him and out of the front door. I knew I couldn't leave them alone, not for long, but I had to do this.

I sprinted as fast as I could manage, ignoring the pain in my womb, the tug of my stitches as I ran to the corner of our road. I stopped, catching my breath, bracing my hands against the wall of the corner shop, waiting for the stitch in my ribs to ease, then pushed the door open and walked inside. The bell gave an irritating little tinkle as I entered and I heard footsteps coming from the back room in response. People always say the worst thing about living in a city is the lack of community. The fact that you can live next door to someone for years, decades even and still be barely more than strangers. Right now, that was something I was grateful for.

I walked up to the counter, facing the woman behind the till. She had messy, dark brown hair and sallow skin which seemed to hang from her bones, and though it was hard to tell, I would have guessed her to be in her early sixties. I had no idea what her name was, or where she was from, her accent was tinged with northern tones, but I was no good at placing their origins. I'd never asked and she'd never offered the information. She looked at me blankly, no trace of recognition, though I'd been in to buy eggs and milk at least thirty times when we'd left it too late to go to the big supermarket. "Yes?"

"Can I have ten B and H Gold please. And a lighter."

She nodded, turning to the cabinet behind her, pushing aside the shutter and grabbing what I'd asked for. She handed the pack and the lighter to me and I passed her a twenty pound note. She handed me back my change, picking up a magazine and turning towards the back room, ignoring me as I left.

The warmth seemed to radiate from the pack in my palm, a homecoming, a welcome. It was like going for an illicit meeting with an ex-lover. You knew it was wrong, that it would open up a whole world of trouble, tear open scars that had long since healed. But you also knew just how good it would feel in the heat of the moment and that was enough to stop you from turning back and being sensible.

I lifted my hand, appraising the packet, surprised to see that the pretty gold packaging I remembered had been replaced with a dark, ugly black and grey cardboard, a huge cataract filled eyeball spread wide across the centre. The whole pack was covered in death threats and warnings. *Killjoys,* I thought, screwing up my face. I ripped off the cellophane, shoving it into the bin beside the curb and flipped the lid, bringing the cigarettes to my nose, inhaling. At least these were the same. The scent brought back so many feelings of security and fun and freedom. They reminded me of a time when I'd been happy. When life had been simple.

I glanced up the road, back to my home, where my children were alone, waiting. I should go back there. I knew it was dangerous to leave them unattended. Anything could happen. I should have brought Milo with me at least. Toby wouldn't move if the TV was on, but Milo... good mothers did not leave their newborn babies home alone. He could be choking on his own vomit right now. Screaming for someone to come. He was so little. I couldn't walk away.

But I couldn't seem to propel my feet forwards either. A sense of terror locked them in place. Because, if I went back now, it was possible – likely even, that *I* would be the biggest threat to their safety. The action replay of Toby's face, eyes screwed tightly shut as his head smashed into the table, the howl of pain as his skin split open played constantly in my mind. *I should leave them. I should go somewhere now and never come back. Nate would come home soon. He'd find them. They would all be better off if I just left.*

I slid a cigarette from the packet, holding it lightly between my thumb and index finger, rolling it gently as I stared at the house in the distance. I brought the smooth cylinder to my lips, holding it between them, still unlit. Everything in me wanted to turn and walk away. I didn't want to go back to that house and feel the things that Milo made me feel. I didn't want to ever be in the same room as him again. But I was the only person standing in his way of hurting Toby.

Nate didn't know. He was blind to what was happening, what had changed in the past few weeks. If I left, it was only a matter of time before he did something that could never be undone. The thought was enough to get me moving in the right direction. Reluctantly, I plucked the cigarette from between my lips, sliding it back into the packet and shoving them into my pocket. And then, knowing I was damned whatever I chose to do, I went back home.

Chapter Fifteen

Nate

"I'm back!" I called, pushing my way through the back door with my shoulder, my hands weighed down with bags filled with a weeks worth of groceries. I lowered them down onto the kitchen floor, then straightened, instantly regretting my loud entrance. Megan would be furious if I'd woken one of the boys from a nap. I walked through to the living room, hearing the sound of the TV before I'd even entered.

Toby was sitting crossed legged, his mouth open as he stared at the screen. There was no sign of Megan. I couldn't help feeling a little annoyed. Meg had always made such a fuss about not using screen time as a babysitter, only ever allowing me to put on educational programmes for Toby, with the agreement that I had to sit beside him so I could talk to him and answer his questions. I'd found it hard to stick to initially, my mum had never put a limit on my viewing during my childhood, she'd rarely put limits on anything I wanted to do, but as time had gone on,

I'd seen the benefits of Megan's strict boundaries and grown to agree with them myself. Which was why, walking in to find Toby alone, watching mindless trash after less than two hours under Meg's care was grating to discover.

"Hey, Tobes," I said, stepping into the room. He didn't even look my way. I sighed, backing out of the room, deciding to let the cartoon finish before I broke the spell. I didn't want a meltdown on my hands just yet. Spotting movement from Milo's travel system in the hall, I gave a grin. "Who's been sleeping?" I asked, walking over and stepping around the huge wheels of the buggy, peering beneath the hood. My smile vanished instantly. Milo was struggling against a polka-dot sheet which had wrapped itself around his head. He was grunting as he flailed his arms uselessly against the material. I reached down, yanking it off of him in one swift motion, picking him up and bringing his face to mine. "Oh, bloody hell, buddy. That was scary!"

He took one look at me and started bawling, thrashing his little fists against my chest, arching his back in rigid protest. I jiggled him in my arms, frowning. Walking to the bottom of the stairs, I called up to Meg. No response. I ran up, still trying to calm Milo, pushing open doors, calling up to the loft room. The place was empty.

Running back downstairs, I went to Toby, crouching down in front of him to get his full attention. He blinked, glassy eyed, slowly focusing on my face. "Hi, Tobes. Do you know where Mummy is?"

"No." He turned his head, trying to see past me to his cartoon and I sucked in a breath. "What happened to your head, Toby?" There was a huge bruise surrounding a weeping cut on his temple, crusted blood beneath it trailing down his cheek. Toby ignored me and I touched his chin, lightly angling his face up to mine until I was sure I had his attention again.

"Toby?"

He nodded.

"What did you do to your head? Did you fall?"

"Mama push," he said, his fingers going to the

wound. "Sore bump," he added.

"What do you mean? Where is Mama? Toby?" He didn't answer. I'd lost his focus again. I stood up, worried now. Where was she? What the hell did Toby mean, *Mama push*? She wouldn't have hurt him. *Never*. I knew my wife and there was no way on earth she would ever lay a finger on him. She'd die before that happened. It had to be some sort of mistake, but where was she? Milo had found his fingers and was sucking at them and I realised I had no idea when he'd last been fed. Megan had been leaving it to me. She'd been leaving everything to me.

I went into the kitchen, unsure what to do first. The ice-cream was melting on the tiles, the underfloor heating slowly ruining everything I'd bought. Milo was hungry, Toby needed a first aid kit and maybe even a trip to A&E and I needed to find Megan. I didn't understand where she could have disappeared to. She had to be close. She wouldn't just leave the boys. She'd been a little strange lately, acting distant and distracted, but even so, to go off without a word? It was impossible.

I opened the back door, looking out into the garden, knowing already that I was wasting my time. I would have passed her on my way in from the garage. Still, I scanned the four corners of the garden from the back step, taking in the pile of fallen leaves from next door's apple tree, the rusty wheelbarrow half filled with murky rainwater.

I stepped back inside, pulling the door closed, ignoring the ball of worry growing in my gut. I walked determinedly through the house towards the front door, opening it and stepping out into the cold, hoping to see her emptying the bins, or chatting to the Postie or even just taking a breath of fresh air. The wind whipped through the holly bushes lining the front wall, the bin lid rattling loudly, the only sound in the deserted front garden. There was no sign of her.

"This is bloody ridiculous," I muttered under my breath, wrapping my free arm around Milo's back, protecting him from the cold. I walked back inside, slamming the door. Her coat was still on the hook beside it. It didn't make any sense. I gritted my teeth, trying to keep my cool, though I could feel my hands beginning to shake. Yanking the phone from its cradle on the hallway table, I pressed the speed-dial for my mum's mobile. It rang twice before she answered.

"Hi, darling!"

"Mum, is Megan with you?"

"No, sweetie, I'm at work."

"Damn it!"

"What's wrong?"

"Nothing... actually, I'm not sure it is nothing. I just got home and she isn't here. I can't find her."

"She's probably just gone down the beach for a walk, love. You were telling her she needed to get out, back to her old self. I'm sure she just – "

"No," I interrupted. "I mean, she's gone without the boys. I just found them here alone!" I could hear the panic in my voice and forced myself to take several deep breaths, trying to calm myself down. There was a long silence on the end of the phone. "Mum?"

"Call the police."

"What?"

"Do it, Nate. Call them now."

"And say what? My grown wife has gone for a walk?"

"Get them out looking for her!"

"Mum, they won't – " A click from behind me cut me off short. I turned wide eyed as Megan stepped through the front door dressed in jeans, flip flops and a thin t-shirt. She was pale and shaking and I was torn between lunging forward to wrap her in a bear hug and screaming at her for scaring the shit out of me. "She's here," I managed to say, my voice croaky with emotion.

I heard the whoosh of breath on the other end of the line. "Thank goodness," Mum said shakily. "Nate – "

"I have to go. I'll call you later, okay?" I hung up without waiting for a response, still staring at Megan. "Where have you been?" I asked, trying to keep my voice calm, though I felt like yelling with everything I had.

"Nowhere." She glanced at Milo, then down to her feet.

"Nowhere?" I repeated coldly. I felt my blood rising, anger swelling in me now. "Megan, I just came home to find Milo and Toby completely unsupervised, one of them with a head wound, the other nearly suffocating in his blankets. I'll ask you again, and I want a fucking answer. Where have you been?"

She ignored my question. "What do you mean, suffocating?" Her eyes flicked to Milo again, this time lingering on his face.

"What? You thought you could just leave a newborn and a toddler on their own and they would manage? Yes, suffocating, Megan. His sheet was wrapped round his face. Do you realise what could have happened if I hadn't come home when I did? Do you understand, Megan?"

She stared at me, her expression blank.

"What happened to Toby? Why is his head cut?"

She gave a shrug and looked back to the carpet. "He fell."

"He said you pushed him."

"No. He fell. Is he okay?"

"You'd know how he was if you'd been here, doing your bloody job! You shouldn't have to ask me, you should know!"

"I'm sorry." Her voice was monotone. No emotion behind her words. For the first time in my life, I felt like grabbing her by the shoulders and shaking her. Anything, so long as it elicited some sort of human response from her. I wanted to shock her into realising what she'd done, because apparently the risk to our newborn's life wasn't enough to do the job.

"Do you want to lose them? Do you want our children taken away and put in care? Because that is exactly what's going to happen if you treat your responsibilities so lightly. They will take our kids, and I will never fucking forgive you if that happens. Not ever, Megan. So I suggest you sort yourself out, and soon, because I am going back to work on Monday and you need to step up and be a good mother to these boys."

I turned from her, leaving her shivering by the door, unwilling to stare into those blank, empty eyes any longer. I wished more than anything that I could have my wife back. The Megan I loved, who could always make me smile, my best friend in the world. I had never felt so lonely in all my life.

Chapter Sixteen

Megan

I never knew it was possible to hate an inanimate object. To loath something with such intensity that all you could picture when you looked at it, was walking over, lifting it high in the air and smashing it as hard as physically possible against the solid floor. Stamping on it over and over again until it was nothing but dust and broken glass and metal. There were a lot of things I didn't know before Milo, though.

I glared at the round, silver face of the clock on the kitchen wall, wanting nothing more than to destroy it, yet knowing it would make no difference. He would leave no matter what I did. Breaking the clock would not pause time to keep him beside me.

Not that I hadn't tried to sabotage his return to work. Oh, I had. It had been my only goal for days now. But nothing had swayed him. My last chance had been three hours before as Nate and the boys had slept. I'd snuck down to the kitchen, choosing a long, sharp knife from the drawer, holding it steady in my hand as I prepared myself, before heading back through the moonlit hallway. I'd been just steps from the front door when a scream had echoed through the house, and moments later, I had seen the glow of the bedside lamp filtering out beneath the bedroom door, and heard Nate's gruff voice calling to me.

I wished I could believe that it was the innocent cries of a hungry baby. That Milo hadn't been lying there, waiting for the perfect moment to wreck my plan. But I knew differently. For a second, my gaze had fallen to the glint of the long blade in my hand and I'd considered an alternative solution if I couldn't slash Nate's tires. I'd stared at it, trembling as Milo's cries grew steadily louder. Then I'd turned, put the knife back in the drawer and gone upstairs, closing the door behind me.

Now, time had all but run out. Nate was leaving me. Us. I couldn't let him go, but I couldn't seem to convince him to stay. I wrapped my hands tightly around the steaming mug of coffee he'd made for me, the heat burning into my palms, the pain almost soothing. It hurt, but I pressed against the ceramic harder, wanting to feel nothing but this, letting it numb my fears and rambled imaginings, if only for a moment.

Nate came into the kitchen dressed in jeans and a grey long-sleeve t-shirt. His company were of the hip, modern ilk, too cool for suits and shiny shoes. He'd shaved, though, and although his eyelids drooped more than usual, he looked happier than he had in days. Happy to be leaving us. Getting out of this house. Away from Milo, even if he wasn't aware of it.

I'd never wished for a career. Never wanted to be one of those women who can do it all, excel at everything, but now, in the face of accepting my new role alone, with no support and no option to quit, I would have cut out my own tongue if it meant I could swap places with my husband. I watched, silently as Nate picked up his coffee, downing it in three gulps, then putting the empty cup into the dishwasher. "Toby's still asleep," he said. "But Milo needs a feed pretty soon. He's in that rocker thing again," he said, not without a tinge of judgement in his tone.

I stared at him, willing him to see what was in

front of his face.

"There's loads of food and I'll try and call you around lunchtime, alright?"

I didn't reply.

"Meg? You'll be alright, won't you?" he said, his eyes pleading, wanting me to give him permission to abandon ship.

"Please don't go."

He sighed. "What are you afraid of?"

I stared into his eyes, shouting the words in my head, wanting him to understand. *Everything. The baby. Myself. What I might do.* But I couldn't tell him any of that. Instead, I shrugged, biting my lip. Nate came around the table, leaning down to press a kiss onto my forehead. "You'll be fine. I have to go, okay?" He gave a sad little smile, then walked out of the room. I heard him saying goodbye to Milo in a singsong, baby talk, then as he opened the front door, his tone changed. I cocked my ear, listening closer. He was talking to someone, letting them come inside. I stood swiftly, moving to the wall beside the kitchen doorway, listening hard.

"I didn't know you were coming," Nate was saying cheerfully. "I'm sure Megan will be pleased. This is her first full day alone with both boys. I'm heading back to the office today."

"Oh, it goes so fast, doesn't it, the paternity leave, I mean. How have you been getting on?"

I knew the voice. It was Cassandra, my midwife. She hadn't been at the birth, but she'd done all my checks through the pregnancy. But why was she here now? Did she know something? Had she discovered something when I was pregnant that would explain my issues with Milo? And if she had, why would she have kept it a secret from me?

"It's been... challenging," I heard Nate reply. "Megan isn't quite... back to her normal self just yet –"

"Cassandra!" I said brightly, stepping into the hallway, interrupting Nate before he could say anymore. "What a lovely surprise." Nate flashed me a bewildered stare, then checked himself.

"Right, well then, I'm already thirty minutes behind schedule, so I'll be off. Don't forget, Milo needs a feed," he added, his eyes meeting mine.

"I'm sure he'll make his wishes heard," Cassandra grinned. "Bye, Nate, good to see you again," she smiled. He gave a nod and left, pulling the door closed behind him. "So," she smiled, turning to me. "Where is the little chap? I'm so looking forward to meeting him at last," she said, clasping her hands together against her chest.

"In here," I said, forcing my face into what I hoped was a bright smile. I led her into the living room and stood by uneasily while she cooed over the baby. "Why are you here?" I blurted out, unable to hold the question in any longer. She rose from a crouch beside the bouncy chair and took a seat in the armchair beneath the window.

"Post natal check," she smiled. We did discuss it on the phone last week. Don't you remember?" I shook my head. "Ah, I don't blame you. It's all a bit of a whirlwind in these early days, isn't it?" She looked up at me, her blue eyes fixed on mine as she waited for a response. I didn't like the way she was looking at me. The questions. It felt like an interrogation where you knew the verdict was long since decided. She flushed a little when the silence continued, and tapped her fingers on the edge of the armchair. "So," she said. "How are you getting on? Any issues?"

I walked across the room, careful not to get too close to the baby, though I could feel his gaze following every step I took. I lowered myself slowly into the seat furthest from Cassandra, wedging myself into the far corner of the sofa.

"We're fine," I managed. Milo began to grizzle, his fists flailing, and I stared at him, sick with the knowledge that I was going to have to feed and hold him in front of this woman. That she would watch my every move, judging, ticking off items on her little checklist. Nate's words from Saturday afternoon spun through my head. *Do you want them to take our children, Meg? Because they will. They'll take them and I'll never forgive you.*

Was that why she was here? To steal them from me? My eyes flashed to the ceiling, above which Toby still slept, unaware of the danger. I willed him to keep sleeping, not to come down here where she might see him, where she might make a grab for him. Cassandra raised an eyebrow, questioning and I realised I'd missed something she said. I blinked, becoming aware that Milo's grizzle had become a full blown cry. Before I could move, Cassandra was on her knees, unstrapping him from his chair, bringing him to her chest. "It's okay," she said. "I don't mind at all. And this way I get to have a cuddle too. Aren't you a beautiful boy," she simpered. "So lovely, such bright eyes. Oh, don't you just love that newborn smell?"

I nodded. "Yes," I said softly. It was true. I adored the smell of newborn babies. But Milo didn't have it. There was no biscuity, fresh aroma on his scalp. It was disconcertingly absent. I couldn't tear my eyes away from this intruder. She held the baby with such authority. Such confidence.

For the first time in ages, I felt a burst of protective fire ignite inside me. I would not let this woman take my children. Not Toby, and not Milo. He was my problem to solve and I would not let her come into my home and take over. I stood suddenly, going to where she knelt, holding out my arms in wordless demand. She passed him to me instantly, a flash of uneasy confusion on her face. Did she know he was damaged? Did she assume I would stand by and let her have him? Well, if she thought I would make it easy for her, she was wrong. Regardless of my feelings for Milo, he was still mine. I would do my duty as a mother.

Cassandra rose to her feet slowly. "Right," she said, moving towards her bag. "Shall I ask you some questions while you feed him then?"

I shook my head, gritting my teeth in what I hoped was a smile. "Actually, I'm going to have to rearrange, Cassandra. Toby needs to get up and we have a... a toddler group to get to." I made a show of looking at the clock. "Can I call you with some other dates and we can figure out another time?"

"Oh, yes of course. I'm glad to hear you're getting out and about already. Good to get back to normal and get some adult interaction, isn't it?"

"I find it helpful," I lied, watching her closely as she picked up her bag. "Do you want me to weigh him before I go?"

"No. I'll stop in at the clinic on the way home from group." I shepherded her to the door, my heart thumping in my chest.

"But you are feeling okay? Coping?" she asked, fixing her expression into a false imitation of a caring friend.

"Never better." I glanced over my shoulder, hearing a noise. Toby was standing at the top of the stairs, his hair messy from sleep, his postman pat pj's rumpled. I stood straight, blocking him from the midwife's view. "Right, I better get on. You know how it is. I'll call you soon."

"Righto. I'll leave you to it. Oh, and Megan, he is a lovely baby. You're very lucky, you know?" She touched my arm gently and I stepped back, breaking the contact immediately. I had no response to offer her. Nothing to say, except that she had no idea what she was talking about. I pressed my lips together, willing her to leave.

"Well, goodbye," she said, finally, her smile a little less warm now.

"Bye," I replied. I shut the front door the moment

she walked through it, then slid both bolts across. I ran my fingers through the keys on the hooks on the wall, finding the one for the deadbolt, shoving it in, turning it with a satisfying click. I leaned heavily against the door, my mouth dry with terror.

"Mama?"

"I'll just be one moment, Toby," I stammered, breathlessly.

"Need it wee," he said, grasping his pyjama bottoms, already tugging them down.

"One minute!" I ran to the back door, checking it was locked. Then I grabbed half a loaf of bread, a bag of popcorn, three apples and a carton of mango juice. I threw them all in the cupboard under the stairs. I grabbed Toby's basket of toys, shoving a few books in it, adding that to the haphazard pile in the closet. Placing Milo back in his bouncy chair, I slid him into the cupboard, then went to fetch Toby.

"Did it wee on carpet," he said sadly as I climbed the stairs.

"Oh. Never mind." I dried him off with the discarded pyjama bottoms, grabbed some fresh trousers, then carried him downstairs, glancing nervously at the door as I passed it. Climbing into the cupboard, I flicked the switch for the bare light-bulb that hung overhead, casting a dim glow across everything. "We're going to play a little game, Toby," I said softly. Then I closed the door behind us.

Chapter Seventeen

Megan

I was losing my last shred of self control. I felt like the walls were pressing ever closer against me, suffocating, the air growing staler by the minute. It carried the lingering stench of soiled nappies. I'd forgotten to bring spares. With every hour that passed in the dusty, claustrophobic closet, I could feel the malevolent pulse of Milo's hatred growing around me, seeping beneath my skin, cloaking the three of us in its darkness. It took all my willpower not to toss him out into the hall, to let them take him and get him away from Toby. *Away from me.* I didn't want him. But I didn't want them to take him either.

Toby had grown bored of the game the moment the food had run out, standing up from his spot on the bare floorboards and making his way to the door, babbling about finding his doll to give her breakfast. I'd blocked his path, refusing to let him out there, where someone might see him. Where he was in danger of being snatched. Stolen from me. He'd given in easily, to begin with, distracted by the novelty of finding his toy basket under the stairs. But then Milo had begun to cry and Toby had grown fearful of monsters lurking in the darkness, in the corners where the light didn't quite reach. He could sense an evil there too, though I was certain he didn't realise it was coming from his own brother.

He'd fought me then, thrashing to get out, screaming and clawing at me. I could feel the angry welt across my cheek, where he'd sunk his fingernails into my skin in his panic. The guilt had been crushing, knowing that I was breaking his trust. That *I* was the one forcing him to stay in a situation he didn't want to be in. For the first time in his life, he was crying out, begging for my help and I was withholding it. Because he didn't understand.

Sometimes, as a mother, you have to make the decision to cause your child pain and trauma because in the long run it will save them from something so much worse. It's a sick kind of logic. One that requires a stomach of steel and the ability to squash down your own feelings, your own fears, and do what needs to be done. It was for his own good. He just didn't realise it.

After a couple of hours in the cupboard, the phone had rang. I'd heard the answer machine click on and then Jane's voice asking if we needed anything. Checking up on us. Ten minutes later, it rang again, though there was no message this time. The same happened three more times. It was her. Jane. I knew it.

Now, I sat rigidly against the plasterboard wall of the closet, both boys having finally cried themselves to sleep beside me. I had never felt so empty. Drained from days and days of fear. Exhausted, yet unable to sleep. Terrified about what would happen next.

The bulb above me fizzed and went out, casting me into darkness, the only light coming from a tiny gap beneath the cupboard door. The house creaked and adjusted around us. Still I didn't move. We had to stay here. We couldn't be seen.

For a moment, the darkness felt almost comforting. I was hidden. Secure. It was like another world, one where we couldn't be reached. But slowly, my other senses began to adjust, heighten, and the confined space transformed.

I could hear my own breathing, thunderous in my ears, other sounds emerging from the recesses of the closet. Bright, startlingly florescent images flashed from nowhere before my eyes. There one second, gone the next. The visions made me claw at my eyes, desperate to erase them from my memory.

My gaze was drawn down, and I gasped, scrambling back as I found myself surrounded by a carpet of rats, their red eyes glinting from matted brown fur. I kicked out at the creatures, but they disappeared into nothingness and my bare feet collided with thin air. I'd barely caught my breath when I saw a window materialise high up on the wall above me. My hands began to drip with sweat as I watched Toby climb onto the high ledge, his arms spread wide as he launched himself into the abyss. Was this Hell? Was I visiting a place where nothing but evil lurked in every direction? This was the place Milo had been sent from. It had to be.

I was cast into darkness once more, shaking hard

as the next bright picture played out in the air before me. Milo. My son. Only it wasn't him. His head was severed from his body, blood pouring from the jagged stump of his neck, but he was very much alive. His cold eyes met mine, piercing and I knew that nothing would ever destroy him. He was so strong. A high, wicked laugh – his laugh – built around me, consuming me, surrounding me, dragging me down into an inescapable nightmare and I screamed, the terror spilling from my lungs as I covered my eyes with my fists.

The closet door flew open with a crash, natural light pouring in, illuminating everything. I squinted, confused, surprised to see Milo still fast asleep in his bouncy chair, Toby peering up sleepily from the blanket on the floor.

"Megan!"

I looked to the doorway. "Jane."

"What on earth is going on? You frightened the life out of me!"

"Did I?"

"You screamed. And you are absolutely filthy. For

goodness sake, what is going on here?"

I glanced at the boys, catching sight of Toby's tear stained face, smeared with dust and dirt. He crawled out of the closet, clambering into Jane's lap. She wrapped her arms protectively around him, shooting me a look of disgust. "Look at the state of you, darling," she cooed, brushing Toby's hair from his eyes.

I crawled out, standing to stretch my legs, my hands still trembling, my heart pounding hard. Nothing seemed real. It was like being dragged from one nightmare to another. The way Jane kept casting judgement over me with silent glares made me anxious. She gave a tut, rolled her eyes in my direction and reached into the cupboard, plucking Milo from his seat, cradling him against her. "I don't understand, Megan. Why were you under the stairs?"

"We – we were playing a game. We had a picnic. I thought it would be... fun."

Jane stared at me, an incredulous expression clouding her features. "He's been crying," she said, shifting Toby on her hip, trying to keep a hold on both of my children.

I shrugged. "A little bit."

"It sounds like the game was far too scary for him. Why were you in the dark?"

"We weren't. Not at first, anyway. The bulb just blew and they were napping so I didn't bother to move them."

"And you were happy to just sit in the dark, eh?" She peered into the cupboard. "It's full of dust. They really shouldn't be messing around in there, Megan. Especially not little Milo. He'll get it on his chest."

I shrugged, watching the way she covertly checked him over. I didn't like it. *I* was their mother, not her. It wasn't up to her what I did with them. She looked up at me, frowning. Her gaze travelled down me and I hid my shaking hands in my pockets. Her voice was softer when she spoke again. Kinder. "You look like you could do with a long soak in the bath yourself. Go on. Go and sort yourself out and I'll see to these two. Nothing a warm flannel can't fix."

"No, Jane. I can't – " I started, the idea of having them out of my sight, too horrible to even consider.

But Jane was a difficult woman to argue with, especially when she had an idea stuck in her head.

"Megan, don't be silly. I'm their grandmother, aren't I? I *want* to do it. Now go. Have a lovely long soak with some of those jasmine bubbles I bought for you, and when you're done, I'll cook us some dinner."

I stared at her with the realisation that I'd lost. She wouldn't back down. I nodded and went to the stairs. I didn't miss the smug smile on her face as she looked down at Toby and Milo in her arms. "I'll give him a bottle, shall I?" she called as she disappeared into the kitchen. I froze, but remained silent, unwilling to give her the satisfaction of hearing me consent to formula. Of having to admit that I didn't want to feed him.

Ignoring her, I ran up the stairs, turning the taps on fully over the bath, leaving the door wide open so she would hear the running water. I grabbed a musty flannel from the laundry basket, dipping it in the water, running it quickly over my arms and face, then tossed it aside. I flipped my hair over my head, wetting it under the running tap. The water was scalding, but I continued until my head was steaming and saturated. I wound a towel around it, stripped off my clothes, put on my dressing gown and turned off the taps. Tiptoeing back to the stairs, I lowered myself down to the top one, listening to the sounds of Jane and Toby talking in the kitchen.

If she thought she could trick me into leaving her alone with them, she was mistaken. She was trying to get rid of me. She wanted them for herself. I bounced on the spot, tapping my fingers on my thighs, wanting nothing more than to rush downstairs and throw her out, to get her away from us for good. She couldn't be trusted. But I knew what would happen if I lost my temper. She would turn it around, make it seem like *I* was the unhinged one. She was clever. Patient. And that was exactly what I needed to be too.

I listened to the sound of Toby's laughter and bit down on the inside of my cheek, tasting blood as I broke open the skin that had barely begun to heal. I let the pain take over, sinking my teeth in deeper, counting down the minutes until Nate would arrive back home. I hoped he wouldn't be late. I needed him. And I hoped more than anything that for once in his life, he would take my side over hers.

Chapter Eighteen

Nate

"I'm telling you, something's not right, Nate."

"Mum, she's already been to the doctor, you know that. It's just baby blues," I replied, exasperated.

"So you're saying you think she's coping? That this is normal?" she exclaimed, her anger resonating through the phone. I could picture the dent between her eyebrows as she lectured me. "I told you the state I found her in yesterday. It's not normal behaviour, Nate!"

"I'm not saying it's normal. I just think you're making it bigger than it needs to be. She needs time."

"She needs support!"

"I'm doing my best, Mum." I glanced through the fogged up windscreen of my car, towards the seven story building I should have been inside twenty minutes ago. But as if anything was that simple. Mum had whispered in my ear as she left last night, telling me to call her first thing, and she'd looked so serious I hadn't dared not to.

I was two days into my first week back and so far I'd achieved practically nothing, unable to focus with my head so filled with worries about the situation at home. Mum had it wrong. It wasn't a lack of concern on my part. I just knew that Mum loved to build the drama far higher than was necessary.

I gripped the steering wheel, trying to make my voice passive and calm. "I'm sorry, Mum, but I don't know what you expect me to do. I can't be there all the time. I'm doing all I can. You're the one who said we needed to push her, give her some space to get to know Milo without me swooping in all the time. And now, you're saying what? I'm leaving her alone too much? I can't win!"

I heard her sigh. "I know, darling. I'm not accusing you of letting her fend for herself. You know I think you're a wonderful father to those boys. But you need to accept help, something both of you struggle with. Honestly, I think she needs to get herself back to the GP and get a second opinion."

"She only went a few days ago. And she said she'll go back next week if she's no better. You're rushing things, Mum. It's not going to be an instant fix. I do appreciate that you're concerned, and I love you for it, but you need to give her time. Let her decide for herself if she needs a doctor. She's not a child."

"No, but she may not be thinking straight. You didn't see her yesterday, Nate. She frightened me."

"She said you overreacted. She was playing with them."

"You didn't see how scared poor Toby was."

"Mum." My tone was crisp now. I hated being put in the middle of their battles. Being asked to choose sides on an unwinnable war.

"Fine. I'll let it go. But if you won't push her to go back to the doctor, at least let me help. Let me take the boys for a couple of hours each day while you're at work. It's too much too soon for her, doing it all by herself."

"You said that was what she needed!"

"I think I was wrong."

"And you have work," I reminded her.

"I'll take some time off. I'm owed loads of holiday. It's not a problem."

"It's a kind offer, Mum. I'm grateful. But I'm pretty sure Megan wouldn't agree to it. Milo's only twelve days old. He needs to be with her."

"I'm not talking about the whole day or anything, Nate. And not as a permanent arrangement. Just a couple of hours a day for a week or two. It's a massive shock to the system, you going back to work, her alone all day with two tiny people who need her for every little thing. I can help. Give her a chance to focus on herself, her... emotions."

I chewed my lip, warming to the suggestion. "It's not a terrible idea," I conceded.

"So you'll ask her?"

"She won't agree. I'm sure she won't."

"Then *tell* her. Convince her. You know you'll all be so much happier if she gets herself back on track. You need more balance. Oh, and while you're at it, Nate, you really need to have a word with her about this feeding situation."

"What do you mean?"

"The nonsense about breastfeeding or expressed milk only. It was all very well and good with Toby, but she's clearly finding it too difficult this time around. I'm sure a big part of the problem is that Milo is constantly hungry, the poor little mite. He near enough took my arm off when I gave him a bottle of formula yesterday. Hungry babies are grouchy babies and I'm sure Megan isn't offering the breast nearly as often as he needs.

"Mum!" I hissed, feeling clueless and embarrassed. Feeding had always been Megan's domain. Something we'd never discussed, and quite frankly, that was how I preferred it.

"Oh, stop it, Nate. You're a grown man, you can't go all funny when you hear your mother say *breast*, for goodness sake!"

"Fine," I sighed. "Get to the point then."

"You need to tell her that there's no shame in quitting. Loads of mothers use formula nowadays. *You* were a formula baby and you turned out just fine, didn't you? More than fine. Megan probably feels like she has to do it because she fed Toby herself. She wants to keep them even, keep up standards, you know? There's such a lot of guilt when it comes to being a mother these days, so many ideals. It's impossible to live up to them all. She's probably worried you'll think badly of her."

"Of course I wouldn't."

"So tell her."

"Fine. I'll tell her."

"Good boy. And it will make it a whole lot easier for me to take them off her hands if he's used to the bottle." I shook my head at the note of victory in her words and said goodbye. Dropping the phone on the passenger seat I leaned forward, resting my head on the steering wheel. I was *not* looking forward to having that conversation with Megan. Not in the slightest.

Chapter Nineteen

Nate

"Are you fucking serious?"

I winced internally, seeing the instant fury that washed over Megan. It was the most animated and engaged I'd seen her in days, but I wasn't sure that was actually a positive thing. She paced across the bedroom now as I held Milo against my bare chest, propping myself up against the pillows on the bed. "Keep your voice down, will you? He's only just gone off."

She flashed me a glare that could kill, then resumed her pacing. I couldn't deny the difference in her since Milo's birth. *My* Megan had been far from perfect. She'd been indecisive, fickle and often pretty lazy. But she'd also been sweet and loving and kind, so much so that all those other things had never seemed to matter. Lately I was seeing a new side to her and I could only hope it was temporary, because I sure as hell didn't want it sticking around.

"Megan," I tried again. "Nothing's been decided. I

haven't gone behind your back."

"*She* has though! This is what she's been building up to. Oh, she thinks she's so fucking clever, going through you to get her own way. She knows how easily she can get you on side. You've never said no to her in your life, have you?"

"On side? There are no sides, Meg. If anything, we're all on *your* side. Mum just wants to help. Give you a chance to take care of yourself, because she sees how hard it is for you with two of them."

"Oh, she sees alright. I know she sees. Never stops watching, does she? Watching and waiting for me to get it wrong. And then what? She can swoop in and be the fucking hero and snatch my children out from under me! She thinks she could do it all so much better than I could ever manage."

"That's unfair, Megan. You know she would never judge you."

Megan slammed the flat of her hand so suddenly against the wardrobe that I jumped, the noise startling as it broke through the silence of the house. Milo stirred in my arms and I stared at her, unable to understand why she was being so unreasonable.

She'd never been a big fan of my mum's interfering and constant presence in our lives, but she'd bitten her tongue as much as possible, knowing how difficult it was for me to be put in the middle. And since Toby was born, they'd found common ground. They'd become, if not close, then friendly. But the way she was talking now, it was as if she hated her, and that wasn't fair. Mum had done nothing to earn such a malicious reaction. Megan glared at me, her cheeks flushed. "She's so wonderful, isn't she? Don't you see, Nate? Can't you see what she's doing?"

I shook my head slowly, dumbstruck at the intensity of her reaction. I hadn't expected the conversation to go well, but I'd never imagined she would get this worked up. I could only presume that it was from the post birth hormones. I felt so far out of my depth I didn't know what to say or do to make it better. Which was *exactly* why I needed her to let mum step in and support us both. Mum wanted to help and we both clearly needed the extra support, so why on earth couldn't Megan seem to accept it? It was obvious that we couldn't continue like this.

She pointed a shaking finger at Milo. "She wants him. Toby. *Both* of them. She wants to take them from me. I won't let it happen. I won't!"

"Darling, that's not true," I said quietly. "But like I already told you, nothing has been arranged or decided. If you really don't want her help, I'll just tell her."

"I want her to leave me the fuck alone. I mean it, Nate, I want her away from this house."

I thought of mum's face if I told her to stop coming over. It would break her. She'd been just mum for as long as I could remember. My dad had walked out when I was a toddler, not bothering to stay in touch, and there had been no boyfriends, no dates, not even any friends since. With the exception of one of the women from the garden centre, who she had lunch with a handful of times a year, Megan, the kids and I were all she had in the world.

Meg *knew* how much she relied on us, how she needed us. I would not cut her out. And neither would she when she'd calmed down. I'd obviously touched a raw nerve. Things would be better in the morning.

I sighed, rubbing at my eye sockets with my fingertips. "I'll talk to her, okay? Everything will be fine. I promise. Now please, will you come to bed?"

"Not yet." She was at the window now, peering out into the darkness. I stood up, careful not to jostle the sleeping baby in my arms, walking slowly around the bed. I lowered Milo into his basket, adjusting his blanket so it was tucked in tightly. I still had sickening flashbacks of finding him in the pram, quietly suffocating in his polka-dot sheet. I double checked that it was secure and straightened up. Megan was staring at me. There was something inexplicable in her eyes that looked like fear, but I couldn't for the life of me think what she had to be afraid of. And I was too tired to ask. I rubbed my eyes again and threw her a weak smile. "What about the breastfeeding?" I heard myself ask. I knew

instantly that I should have kept my mouth shut. Her face darkened, her eyes narrowing, the fear replaced with fury. "You mean, will I stop breastfeeding to make it more convenient for your mother to take him from me?"

"No – I..."

"How I choose to feed him is not your concern. And it's certainly not hers!" she spat, her voice growing steadily louder. "Do you understand me?" she shouted.

"Meg, you'll wake him."

"Stop telling me what to do! Stop controlling me! I'm so sick of this. You can't see what's right in front of your eyes! You might as well tear them out because you never bloody use them!"

I felt my jaw drop as I stood in silence, absorbing the venom coated words. She had never been so cruel. So vicious. Finally, I spoke. "You clearly need some space, so let me give it to you. I'll sleep in the loft room." I turned from her, heading for the door, pausing as I passed Milo, wondering if I should take him with me. If I even trusted her to look after him in this mood. It was the first time I'd ever felt truly uneasy about her ability to be a good mother and it shook me to the core. I began to reach for his basket, but Megan's voice came from close behind me, cold and flat, the anger replaced with something far more frightening.

"Leave the baby," she said. I looked at him sleeping in his basket and squashed down my uncertainty, nodding once then leaving the room, sad to realise that the one emotion I felt over all others as I ascended the stairs to the loft, away from my wife, was relief.

Chapter Twenty

Jane

I made my way around the side of Nate's house, peering through windows as I passed, pausing only briefly at the back door. There was no sign of Megan or the children. I couldn't pinpoint why I felt so tense. Nate had called on his way into work thirty minutes before to tell me that they both appreciated my offer to babysit in the afternoons, but that Megan wasn't ready to have them away from her. And then he'd told me she needed some space. *From me*. He hadn't said it, but I knew it was what he meant. I would have loved to be a fly on their wall as he'd presented my offer last night, seen the way she reacted. She was being unfair. Trying to leave me out, when I knew she needed help. She was so stubborn. Give her space? Leave her to make a mistake, more like.

I dipped my hand into the depths of my bag, rummaging in the side pocket and pulling out a handful of dry roasted peanuts, shoving them into my mouth and chewing fast. I'd come straight over after

Nate's call, determined to convince Megan to change her mind, missing breakfast in my haste. Now my stomach rumbled loudly, protesting at this unwelcome change in my routine.

I wondered if I was being too pushy. Was it possible that I was becoming one of those overbearing, in your face mother-in-laws women were always lamenting about? That they saw me as the problem rather than the solution? I swallowed the nuts and wiped my mouth on the sleeve of my coat. It was a question I would have to save for another time, because as much as she needed her space, I needed to know that she was taking care of my precious grandsons. I wouldn't stand back and watch her mess it up. I would be there for them, no matter what. No matter how unpopular it made me with my daughter-in-law.

I tried the handle, surprised when I found it locked. Megan never locked the back door and now I'd found it in this unwelcoming state twice in the past three days. Her new found obsession with keeping people out made me uneasy. "No matter," I muttered, reaching into my bag again.

I'd had a set of keys cut right after Nate had moved into the place. Not just for the back door, but the front too. I wanted to be useful. To be able to offer help if he ever needed it. I could nip over and grab a forgotten passport if he found himself stranded at the airport on route to his holiday. I could pop dinner on the stove if he was having a busy day. And every now and then, I could sneak in when I knew the house was empty, and hold Nate's pillow, drinking in the scent of my big, grown up boy, letting myself go back in time to a place where it was just me and him and I didn't have to share him with another woman.

Nate knew about the key, of course. Not that I'd told him, but he'd figured it out pretty quickly after he'd moved in. It wasn't as if I tried to hide it. I would often pop in to do the dusting while he was at work, back before Megan had come to live with him. I'd had to be more discreet after that, but I still let myself in most days. Nate had finally confronted me after I'd rearranged his sock drawer, folding and pairing until everything had been in order. I hadn't been able to resist. Megan didn't seem to consider it part of her role. In fact, anything resembling housework seemed to fly under her radar.

I hadn't tried to hide the fact that I'd been taking care of things. And Nate, to his credit, had never asked me to hand back the keys. I think he liked knowing I would always be able to come when he needed me. And besides, he knew I would only go and get another set made. I had plenty of copies at home. They had long since given up bothering to lock the back door, always leaving it open, ready for my arrival. Until this week.

I frowned as I looked at the door, wondering what to do. I could let myself in again. The only issue now was Megan. I was sure Nate wouldn't have mentioned that I had a key and if she knew, she wouldn't like it. And the state she'd been in lately, I would probably scare the life out of her, sneaking in like a robber. But, if I knocked, she might not answer. And I *had to* get inside. I had to see those babies for myself. There was nothing for it. I slid the key into the lock, hearing the soft click, and pushed open the door. Treading quietly, I stepped into the kitchen, pulling the door shut behind me. Megan's voice drifted through the house, her words coming fast and angry. I sighed, hoping she wasn't remonstrating at those poor children. She'd been so hard on Toby lately. I couldn't bear the thought of seeing his little bottom lip wobble as it always did when he thought he'd done something he shouldn't have.

I considered calling out, shouting hello, making my presence known, but something stopped me, my words sticking in my throat. Instead, I trod lightly, following the sound of her voice upstairs. They were in Toby's bedroom.

Megan was still talking, so fast that there was no possibility for Toby to cut in. He was far too young to be given a lecture like this. I came up beside the open doorway, stopping to listen. Her words were so fast I couldn't make any sense of them. It sounded like she was in the midst of a heated argument, and it dawned on me that she might be speaking on the phone, rather than directing her venom at poor little Toby. I could hear the ping of his little toy toaster and smiled. He loved to make pretend little meals and watch as you "ate" his offerings. I could spend hours role playing if he'd let me.

I listened, unsure what was stopping me from going into the room. I was supposed to be here to offer help, not to snoop and eavesdrop. Still, I didn't move.

I was suddenly aware that Megan had stopped talking. I could hear Toby saying "Toast for you, Milo!" and I pictured his joy as he shared with his new brother. Such a good, sweet child, just like his daddy had been. "Mama," Toby continued. "Toby maked Milo toast."

I grinned, loving the way he spoke about himself in the third person.

"Do you like him?" I heard Megan ask. "Do you like having a brother?" I swallowed thickly. Toby didn't reply. Megan continued to push for an answer. Why? Was she feeling guilty? Sad for Toby who had lost his position as only child, only son?

"Do you wish we could send him back where he

came from?" she asked.

"No, Mama," Toby replied. I breathed out, relieved, hoping his answer would help Megan to relax. To finally accept that this was her life now. Milo was *her* responsibility, and Toby would adapt to all the changes that came with having a sibling. I waited to hear if Megan would respond. If the heavy weight that seemed to press on her every word, making her voice flat and lifeless would lift, even a little bit. Instead, when her words finally came, they were the opposite of what I had hoped to hear.

"I do," she said softly. "I wish we could get rid of him. I wish we could go back to how things used to be."

I stepped round the door-frame, my anger flaring as I glared at her. She was sitting beside Toby on the carpet, her face blank as she looked up at me. "Megan!" I exclaimed. "I cannot believe you would say such a terrible thing!"

Megan rose slowly to her feet, her eyes never leaving mine. Very deliberately, she stepped in front of Toby, blocking him from my view. "How did you get inside?" she asked.

"The back door. Like always," I blustered, annoyed at having to explain myself when *she* was the one in the wrong.

"I locked the back door."

I shook my head. "Nope, it was open." I saw the confusion cross her face and felt a brief surge of guilt at my lie. "And," I continued, placing my hands on my hips, "I heard what you said just then. It's not on, Megan. You can't have favourites!"

"Easy for you to say. You only have one."

I felt the blood drain from my face and gripped the door-frame for support. *Not her fault,* I reminded myself. She couldn't know how deep her words cut. I breathed in through my nose, steadying myself. I was here to help, for the sake of the boys, and that was exactly what I would do.

"Megan, love, you look done in. Look, I know you said you wanted a bit of space, but you're clearly having a hard time of it. There's no shame in accepting help. Why don't I take Toby and Milo to mine for a few hours and Nate can pick them up on his way home from work?" I smiled, trying to get her on side.

"Shouldn't you be at work?"

I shook my head. "I've taken some time off, actually. I was well overdue a holiday, and I would much rather be helping you." I could already picture it now, the busy house, the baby snuggled in my arms as I prepared lunch, Toby chattering away as he role played, absorbed in the stories he dreamed up. Everyone says the best thing about being a grandparent is that you get to give them back. I couldn't disagree more. I hated that part – loathed handing them over at the end of my allotted time slot. There was nothing in the world I loved more than having them all to myself. The thought of taking both of them together filled me with unspeakable joy. And if Megan needed the support, it was win-win.

As I watched, it seemed as if a mask lowered over Megan's face. One second, she was staring at me with blank, haunting eyes, the next it was as though the clock had reversed two weeks and the Megan I knew and recognised had materialised before me. Her eyes focused in on me, a warm, wide smile spreading across her face. "That's very kind of you, Jane," she said. "But it won't be necessary. I'm fine. Absolutely fine. And we have a busy afternoon planned." She stepped forward, ushering me out of the room and I was so stunned I let it happen, moving back as she crowded into my personal space.

"Megan," I stuttered. "Don't be silly. Let me help."

"You'll be the first person I call if I need it," she smiled. "But right now, we're fine. As I said." She walked behind me, giving me no choice but to go down the stairs, following me all the way to the back door. "Thanks for popping round," she said, still smiling. It was disconcerting. My stomach twisted uncomfortably. She opened the door, looking at it pointedly. I stepped outside and turned to face her.

"Bye, Jane." She pushed the door closed and I heard the turn of the key, her eyes on mine through the glass panels, a silent communication. *You aren't welcome.* She gave a stiff wave and turned her back on me. I stared after her, watching her shadow disappear as she walked away. Shakily, I turned, stepping off the back door step. I made it three paces across the garden before I fell to my knees and vomited into the rose bush.

Chapter Twenty-One

Megan

How dare she! That woman, that fucking woman, was unbelievable. Sneaking her way into my home like a snake, spying on me, never relenting in her ever persistent goal. I raced upstairs, furious at having been forced to leave Toby alone with Milo in order to escort Jane out, but for once it had been the safer option. I had seen the intent in her eyes. The desire.

I rushed into Toby's room, glancing around, checking for changes. Both Toby and the baby were exactly where I had left them. I should have felt relieved, but the anger and betrayal was still flowing through my every pore, making my limbs shake with the need to lash out. I wanted to hit *her*. That woman. I hated her for what she was trying to do. I pushed the bedroom door closed, sealing us inside, the uneasy feeling of being spied on, watched, lingering over me.

"I can't live like this anymore," I said out-loud, throwing my head back with force against the solid wooden panels of the door. The pain was satisfying. If only for a few seconds, it blocked out everything else. I flung my skull back again, hissing as the hard surface collided with skin and bone. "What am I going to do? What am I going to do? I can't keep going like this. I can't. I can't. I can't."

I let my face drop to my hands, breathing hard, feeling the way the panic filled my lungs making every breath more difficult than the last.

"Kill him, Mama."

I lifted my face, blinking. "What?"

"Kill the baby. Make him go away."

I stared at Toby, my lips dry, a swollen mass in my throat preventing me from swallowing. I didn't understand. "You... you didn't say that. Did you, Toby? Did you say it? No... No you can't have. You wouldn't know how. I must be imagining... not real. It can't be real," I breathed, staring hard at his face, watching his tiny mouth form words he would never say. My mind had to be playing tricks on me. I was so tired, so very tired. It had to be a mistake.

I crouched down in front of him, my face inches

from his as I reached out, gripping his arm hard. "Tell me!" I demanded. "Say it again. Tell me!" His eyes met mine, earnest and innocent.

"Mama, you kill the baby. Kill Milo."

I gasped, releasing his arm, falling backwards onto the carpet. "Is this real?" I whispered, staring into his round, bright eyes, hoping to understand why he was telling me such awful things. How could this be happening? How could he tell me to do that?

I glanced over at Milo. He was fidgeting in the bouncy chair. Always strapped in and secure, tied up safely because I still couldn't trust myself not to cave his head in with my foot. I didn't want to admit the thoughts that Toby's words had triggered. It was too awful. I knew I could never share the darkest corners of my mind with anyone. Not ever. I knew they would never understand.

But the truth was, as much as I resisted it, I knew that I'd been building to this moment for a very long time now. I'd known from when he was just a few days old that something was very wrong with him. That eventually, somehow, he would have to go. Toby was right. If Milo died, everything would be okay again. Toby would be safe. Milo couldn't hurt him. Jane wouldn't have such a hold over us. With a sickening knot in my stomach, I realised I was actually considering it.

"How?" I heard myself whisper. Could I really do it? Kill a baby, no matter how dark his soul? Could I end a life?

Toby smiled widely and pointed to the window and I nodded, the puzzle pieces all coming together. *Of course*. It all made sense now. The vision in the closet. Toby had climbed up to the ledge and with a grin on his face, jumped out. It had been as though he were flying. Quick. Painless. I looked at Milo. It would be as easy as letting go. Over so fast, he would never even realise he was falling. A kindness, really.

"Yes," I murmured. "You're right. I have to be strong now. Only *I* can end this. Nobody else has the strength to let him go, he's got too deep beneath their skin. It *has to* be me." I stood, moving with fresh determination towards Milo, unstrapping him from his chair, lifting him up. He rooted, his mouth sucking at thin air, but I ignored his demands for food. His hunger would be over soon enough.

I carried him towards the window, feeling like I was only half present. It was like a dream... a nightmare. I couldn't be sure what was real, but I knew this was the only choice. There was no other way for our family to move forward. I looked to Toby for reassurance, needing his support and he smiled. Nodded. Pointed. He was so wise. So brave. He knew why we had to do this. He could see. I hadn't realised it to begin with, but now it was so clear. He knew the difficult things that had to be done. I was so glad he was with me, that I didn't have to go through it alone.

I sucked in a breath and pushed open the window, stepping closer. The cold air crept into the room, snaking around us. I peered down to the hard ground below. The bedroom was at the front of the house, the driveway directly beneath the window. There were no soft bushes to break his fall. He was so tiny. This would work. It *had* to work. I needed it to be over.

Milo strained in my arms and I held him tighter, not daring to look at his face. I couldn't. He would manipulate me. Change my mind. I couldn't let it happen. I grasped him in one arm, ignoring the tiny cry that rang out, and stepped up onto the narrow wooden windowsill.

I could go too. I bit my lower lip, tasting blood. It was a possibility. I could jump. The relief would be so immense. To finally quiet the constant terror in my mind. To have nothing but an eternity of silence. But as I looked down now, I realised it wouldn't work. The fall wouldn't be enough to kill me. *No.* It had to be just him.

I grasped the edge of the window-frame, leaning out as far as I dared. There was a lightness inside me now. Soon, I would have my life back. I would no longer have to live in the shadow cast by Milo's wickedness. I'd never have to feel him suckle at my breast, knowing I was nourishing a monster, again. It would all be over.

He was crying harder now, and despite myself, I looked down. His face was red, his eyes scrunched up as tears leaked from the corners trailing down to his rosebud mouth. My heart thumped rapidly against my ribs. My head was filled with noise. *So much noise.* I felt a tug on the bottom of my jeans and looked down. "Toby?"

He was crying too. Scared. Why was he scared? I didn't understand. It made me feel frightened again. He rubbed the top of his arm and I focused in on the red mark spread across his pale skin. Had *I* done that? Had I hurt my son? My sweet Toby? I hadn't meant to. And why was he crying so hard when I had seen him smiling, telling me what I had to do just moments before? I didn't understand.

"Mama," he whimpered. "Cuddle. Cuddle me, Mama," he sobbed.

"But – but what about Milo? The window? I'm supposed to... I was going to..."

Startling even myself, I let out a roar, animal and horrified as I looked down at my children. "Oh my god. Oh god, oh god!" What was I doing? What had I almost done? This wasn't sane! It was wrong. So wrong. Something was broken inside me. There was no other explanation.

"Milo," I gasped, awareness filling me, terrifying as

I looked around, aware of my precarious position at the ledge of an open window. It was like waking from a long sleep to find yourself balancing on a cliff edge. I jumped down to the bedroom carpet, holding him tightly, my entire body trembling. I could have *killed* him. A baby. *My* baby.

The tears that had been locked inside for so long fell fast now, streaming in hot rivulets down my cheeks, stinging, blinding. I wasn't fit to take care of them. And everyone knew it. Jane had been right, I was an unfit mother. I had let them both down and now I would have to make up for it.

I kissed Milo's forehead, and then Toby's, tasting the mixture of our combined tears. "I'm sorry," I sobbed. "Mummy is so sorry."

I had known that this would end in death. But now, I knew, it wasn't Milo's. It was *mine*. Because the only way to save my children's lives, was to end my own.

Chapter Twenty-Two

Nate

"Sir?"

"I'm sorry, what?"

"I asked if you'd like it toasted?"

"Oh right. Yeah... Yes, toasted please."

The girl nodded and turned her back on me as she prepared the sandwich. She wrapped it in greaseproof paper and handed it to me with an expectant look on her face. I stared blankly at her, noticing the thick black eye-liner running along her eye-lid, a gooey black mass collected in a snotty ball in the corner of her eye. I wondered if she knew it was there and didn't care, or if nobody had told her. "Three pounds fifty," she said, leaning towards me, enunciating each word slowly as if this wasn't the first time she'd asked. Perhaps it wasn't.

I couldn't seem to think straight lately. Josh at work had laughed and said something about sleepless nights and the trials of newborn parenting, but I couldn't remember it being like this with Toby. I'd woken several times this past week to find Megan missing from the bed, though the children were sound asleep. Each time, I'd found her doing something so utterly bizarre that I hadn't known how to react.

Last night, I'd lay awake in the silence of the loft room, not wanting to head back into our bedroom, and no doubt into another fight, yet unable to sleep, worrying about that unsettling emptiness she'd had in her eyes when she'd spoken about my mother. Even in her worst moods, our nastiest arguments, I'd never seen her like that. So cold. It was as if she'd changed into a whole new person, and the Megan I knew didn't exist anymore. I was beginning to think I was underestimating how bad things were. Maybe she was ill after all. Depression could play havoc with your mind. Maybe it *was* more than just the baby blues. I'd finally fallen into a fitful sleep long after midnight, resolved to book another appointment at the doctors before the end of the week if she was no better.

I'd only been asleep a few hours when I'd been jolted into consciousness, aware of a loud banging coming from downstairs. The clock on the bedside table read four a.m. I'd rushed out of bed, bursting through the door to find the living room in complete disarray. She'd upended the sofa, emptied the bookshelves, the whole place had looked like a crime scene. When I'd asked her what she was doing, she'd told me she was looking for Toby's cuddly bunny.

She'd said it so calmly, so sure of herself that I'd assumed he'd woken asking for it, but when I'd joined the search, tiptoeing into his bedroom with the intention of looking under his bed, I'd found him sound asleep, the bunny smiling up at me with its big black glassy eyes, tucked beneath Toby's chubby forearm. Megan had seemed just as surprised as I was when I'd pointed it out to her.

She was overtired. Hormonal and adjusting to life as a mum to two children. This sort of thing was just a consequence of this difficult new phase as we figured out how to be a family of four. That's what I kept telling myself as her behaviour grew stranger and increasingly out of character. But even as I took my change and picked up the sandwich, I felt the rolling wave of nausea in the pit of my stomach, the clammy grip of fear as I wondered if it could be something bigger. Something which sleep and time alone couldn't solve.

It was Wednesday and I'd only been back from paternity leave since Monday morning, but even so, I'd decided to take a longer lunch break and pop home to see what I could do to make things easier for Meg. Mum had been on my case even more than usual, calling me constantly throughout the day while I was trying to catch up on the work I'd missed, to ask after her and the baby.

It was always *"How's Megan?"* She'd stopped bothering to ask after *my* well-being. It was distinctly unlike her. She'd *always* been concerned with how I was doing. Megan called it coddling. Smothering. But I'd never complained. I would never have admitted it, but the truth was, I liked it. It made me feel special. Protected. Megan couldn't understand it, but then she'd had both parents growing up. Granted, they weren't close, but she'd still had both of them. Her dad hadn't abandoned her, leaving one parent to overcompensate. I appreciated my mum for making that extra effort. But this past week, every time we spoke, I'd felt close to screaming, *"You know, I'm tired too, Mum! What about the father? What about me?"*

I hated to admit it but I was actually jealous. Jealous that Meg was getting all my mum's attention. And that was pretty sick. A grown man, unwilling to share his mummy. *What a ridiculous notion.* I knew I needed to pull myself together and admit that Megan was going through something I didn't necessarily understand, but maybe my mum did. I needed to be there for her, even though I was shattered too. So, I'd pushed back the telephone conference I was supposed to be taking after lunch, bought her favourite cheese and rocket sandwich from the little tea-shop we liked to visit on rainy Sundays, and jealous or not, bone-tired or not, I was going to step up and do whatever I could to make her day easier.

I drove home in thoughtful silence, parking diagonally across the driveway and looking up at the house, noting that the upstairs curtains were closed. Maybe by some miracle, she'd managed to get the boys to nap at the same time and was getting some rest herself. As quietly as I could, I pushed open the front door, hearing immediately that I'd been wrong about the nap.

The screams of both children rang shrilly through the house from upstairs. There was something intense and panicked in their cries that stopped me in my tracks. An eerie desperation that had my blood running cold. I dropped the sandwich, running towards the pale blue carpeted stairs, taking them two at a time. The boy's bedroom door was closed, and I could hear the terror in Toby's voice as he screamed, "Mama, Mama, Mama!" over and over again.

"I'm coming Toby!" I yelled. "I'm here, buddy. *Shit!*" I pushed against the door but it wouldn't budge. Only then did I notice the shining silver glint of the shed lock bar I'd been keeping in the kitchen drawer, ready to replace the old one in the garden. It was roughly screwed onto the white glossy wood at a haphazard, slanted angle, a heavy padlock running through its centre, sealed shut. There was no sign of a key. "What on earth..." I muttered, confusion and panic fogging up my thoughts.

My hands shook as I grasped the padlock, pulling at it fruitlessly. The blood roared in my ears, competing with the children's screams which were reaching a horrendous crescendo now. I could hear Milo sucking in huge gulps of air, working to breath through his despairing sobs. He was struggling. What if he vomited? What if crying that hard caused him to have some sort of seizure? I *had to* get in there.

"Boys!" I called through the door, hearing the edge in my voice. "Daddy's here. I'm coming. I'll be right there. Toby, where is Mummy? Where's Mama? Is she in there with you?" I could hear him on the other side of the door, making little scratches with his half-moon fingernails as he screamed without pausing, his little throat hoarse. I hated to think how long they'd been in there. "Megan!" I called, my voice echoing through the house. "Meg, where the fuck are you!"

She couldn't be in there with them. Not if she'd locked it from the outside. "Come on, Nate. Think!" I muttered roughly. "Toby? Toby calm down, buddy. Where's Milo? Is he near the door?" There was no response, just more unintelligible screaming from both of them. It sounded like Milo's cries were coming from near the back of the room. Maybe I could do this. "Toby," I tried again. "Move back from the door, okay? Daddy needs you to move back." If he gave me enough space, I could kick it open. I was certain of it. I could tear down this whole house right now, with the amount of adrenaline pumping through my veins.

"No! No, Dada!" Toby wailed, his words coming in a high pitched shriek.

"Toby, please, I need to get you out, I need your help. You can help Daddy, can't you Tobes?" At that the cries grew even louder and I realised I would never be able to reason with him in this state, he was too scared and upset to cooperate, he wasn't even two and I was asking so much of him.

"Fuck!" I murmured under my breath. "Megan! Where are you?" I grabbed the padlock, shaking it roughly. My fingers brushed against something and I realised that beneath the lock, blue-tacked to the door was a small rectangular piece of paper. I yanked it up, tearing the edge in my haste. The handwriting was Megan's, but the letters fell over one another, jostling for space, the words cramped on the page.

Had to keep them safe. Locked inside. Flushed key down the toilet. Don't let them out. Not until I'm gone. They are safe now. I can't get to them.

It was gibberish, but that was worse than if it had made sense. She'd lost it. What had she done? "Megan!" I yelled again, rushing into our bedroom. It was empty. I threw open her wardrobe expecting to find it stripped of her belongings, but it was still crammed full of artsy skirts and jogging bottoms and knitted sweaters. I braced myself against the door frame, shaking. I realised that I could no longer hear Milo crying. But in place of newborn wails, I could hear something new.

The haunting strains of classical music drifting down from the loft room above. The room that we only ever used to store boxes and put up occasional guests, despite the fact that we'd done it up intending it to be our master-suite. We'd never bothered to move up there. The window was south facing and it was always too hot in the summer months, too bright in the mornings. We'd kept it empty, save for the spare double bed, thinking we'd use it as a playroom when Toby was older. Sometimes Megan did yoga up there, or took a candlelit bath in the en-suite, but she couldn't be doing that now. Unless she was stripping the sheets after I'd slept up there last night. But why the music? The note? It didn't make sense.

Now that I heard the music, I wondered how I could have ever missed it. It sounded like violins, or string instruments at the very least. Not the kind of music we listened to. I didn't know we even had anything like it in our collection.

Every instinct in my body told me not to put my foot on the bottom step. Not to go up there. But I knew I had to. I had to find her. I ran up the stairs, bursting into the bright, clean room. I ran across the perfectly unmarked cream carpet to the far corner or the room, pausing at the closed door of the en-suite. Behind it, from inside the bathroom, the music was almost deafening. "Megan?" I called, hearing the tremor in my voice. "Meg?" I pushed the door and it swung open. I could hear screaming, but this time I couldn't tell if it was me, the children or just the thunderous sound of panic roaring in my ears.

Blood coated every surface of the bathroom. It ran down the white tiles above the sink. It was splattered against the frosted window and smeared over the walls. The bath was filled to the brim, the water stained a deep scarlet, and with her head lolling lifelessly against the back rim, Megan lay, still clutching the kitchen knife.

For a second, everything seemed to stop. My eyes scanned the room, trying to make sense of what I was seeing, to understand. My gaze travelled over her pale face, the eyelids tinged with blue from a series of sleepless nights, the lips almost the same shade of lilac blue, slightly open. I made myself look away. I didn't want to see her like this. My gaze moved to the knife in my wife's hand, the blood still shimmering on its blade.

"It's still wet!" I gasped, a sudden wave of hope

washing over me. I lurched forward, grasping her beneath the armpits, dragging her bloody and naked from the bathtub, out of the horror scene of the bathroom and into the loft room where Toby's cries were still echoing frantically from his locked room below.

I felt like I wanted to tear myself in half. *The tool box!* I thought suddenly. I needed to get the tool box. I could unscrew the lock-bar. Get in there. But there was no time, not yet. I lay Megan on the carpet, trying to assess the damage. Blood smeared in ugly, irregular patches on the once pristine carpet. "Megan!" I yelled, shaking her shoulders. Her right wrist was cut, a long smooth gash running three inches or so along the line of the vein. There was too much blood to tell how deep she'd cut.

I grasped her wrist between my palms, squeezing tight to stem the flow of the bleeding. Her left wrist remained unmarked. I wondered if the shock of the first cut had made her pass out. Her blood ran hot and sticky against my palms, but I didn't let go. I leaned forward to check her pulse and my heart flipped in my chest as I saw the unmistakable flicker of her eyelids. I grasped her chin tilting it, making sure her airway was clear. "Meg, Meg baby, can you hear me?" I cried, wiping at my hot tears with blood smeared palms.

She struggled to focus on me. "N-Nate?"

"I'm here. I'm right here."

She stared at me with a bewildered look on her face. Her free hand came up to touch my cheek. "Please..." she said, her voice barely a whisper. "Don't. Don't save me." Her eyes rolled back into her head and her hand fell away from my face.

"No! No, no, no! Don't you dare!" I shouted. My heart was beating hard enough to explode, my hands shaking with terror as I saw her fading away from me. I jumped up, grabbing a towel from the back of the bathroom door, running back to her and wrapping her in it tightly. I ripped my shirt open, shining grey buttons flying everywhere. I pulled it from my body and rolled it, grabbing Megan by the arm and tying the makeshift bandage tightly around her wrist.

Then I yanked my phone from my pocket and

pressed the emergency call button. I wasn't letting her go. No fucking way.

Chapter Twenty-Three

Nate

I swerved the car into the narrow space in the hospital car park, the wheel slick with sweat as I yanked it sharply to the left. I was in no state to be driving, but I'd had no choice. The ambulance had arrived within minutes of me calling, though it had seemed like forever, the paramedics carrying my wife off in a flurry of oxygen masks and activity. They hadn't been willing to wait for me to accompany them and I'd had the boys to deal with.

I hadn't even watched them drive off before I'd been on the move again, searching the kitchen with unhinged desperation for the screwdriver I needed to get into their room. Two police officers had arrived just as I found the right one, running up the stairs behind me. The silence coming from inside Toby's room was so much worse than the screams. I hadn't been able to keep the screwdriver from sliding off the head of the screw, my hands had been shaking so hard.

The female police constable had taken it from me, removing the lock bar with a practised hand and pushing open the door. The two of them had pushed past me without waiting. I'd been frozen with fear at what I saw. Toby was laying face down on the carpet.

"This one's asleep," the stocky PC with the Freddy Mercury moustache said, crouching down beside him.

"And the baby?" I asked.

"Here," the female called from beside the cot. It had been shoved up beside the window, away from it's usual spot by the wardrobe. Her eyes were wide, concerned as she bent down, her movements fast and efficient. My limbs found their strength and I ran forwards. His breathing wasn't right. It sounded forced, his lips a pale pink rather than their usual cherry red, and I saw the cause of his struggle at once. The cord from the blind was wrapped loosely around his neck, not tight enough to cut off his air supply completely, but enough that he was having to work hard.

The PC unwound it, lifting him up to her face. "He's breathing, he's okay," she said briskly, passing him to me. The colour returned quickly to his face and he let rip with a wail that could have brought me to my knees with the relief of it. For the second time in his short life, my wife had neglected her duties so horrifically that she'd nearly caused his death. Anger bubbled inside me at what we could have found, what I would be seeing now had we been even a few minutes later.

"Dada!" Toby squealed, woken by the noise of his brother. He jumped up, running at me, his face swollen and tear stained, and my legs buckled as I held my boys tightly in my arms, my sobs ragged as I breathed in the smell of them.

"Are you okay?" I asked, checking him over, touching his face softly. "Toby, are you alright?"

"I scared," he said sadly. "I got a sore bruise." He tapped the soft part of his upper arm and I saw the unmistakable fingerprints where he'd obviously been grabbed. I was suddenly very aware of the two constables looking my way.

"She wouldn't have done it on purpose. She's not like that," I said, unable to meet their demanding gazes.

It had taken a further two and a half hours before I'd been able to leave, having had to give a detailed statement, then repeat it all over again for the benefit of the more senior police who arrived, call my mum so she could come and get the boys and then wait longer still, so that the police could take photographs of Toby's bruises before they were finally satisfied. Even then, there had been talk of social services and they had grilled my mum almost as much as they had me. I knew this was far from over. *What the hell had Megan done?* I didn't know how I would ever begin to forgive her for today.

"If she's even alive," I whispered now, locking the car and making my way towards the entrance for A&E. My legs felt like they'd been dipped in concrete. I didn't want to walk inside that building. To be told that I no longer had a wife. I wanted to drive to my mum's house and listen to her words of comfort, her promises that it would all be okay as she plied me with hot tea and home-made pie, her cheery fire roaring in the grate as Toby played with his trains. I wanted her to fix this like she always did. To make it all okay. But she couldn't. Not this time.

I swallowed hard, pushing my way inside, glancing around at the throngs of people gathered everywhere. People pushing drips. Lying on stretchers. Arguing loudly. A woman rifled through some papers at a semi-circular desk and I approached her quickly. "Excuse me?" I said. " I'm trying to find my wife. She was brought in by ambulance."

"End of the hall, turn right," she said, not looking up. I followed her directions, finding myself at yet another desk of exactly the same design. "Hello, I'm looking for my wife."

"Name?"

"Uh, Nate. Nate Taylor."

The woman gave a slow sigh, as she fixed me with a look of contempt. "Your wife's name."

"Oh. Megan. Her name is Megan Taylor. She was brought in by ambulance."

The woman gave a short nod. "Wait here." My heart seem to just stop for a moment, the breath catching in my throat, before the painful thud of it restarting made me grip the desk for support. Who had she gone to get? Someone to tell me I was too late? That they'd done all they could but it wasn't enough? That I should have called sooner?

My knuckles turned white against cream MDF. I couldn't picture Megan smiling. Laughing. I couldn't picture her any other way than she'd been when I'd dragged her from that bathtub. That image was all I could see, every time I closed my eyes. Branded in my memories forever. My mouth went dry as I heard footsteps approaching. She couldn't be gone. She just couldn't.

"Mr Taylor?"

"Is she alive?" I heard myself whisper. I opened my eyes to find a woman in a pair of grey slacks and a pale blue blouse standing in front of me. She looked like exactly the kind of person who would be sent to deliver bad news, her soft blonde bob and wide blue eyes non-threatening and homely.

"If you could follow me, please?"

"Is my wife alive!" I yelled, slamming my palm on the desk, the echo ricocheting in the silence that followed. The woman gave the briefest of flinches before the mask of serenity descended over her pretty features once again.

"Yes. Your wife is alive. But she *is* rather unwell, so if you could follow me, perhaps we could talk somewhere a little more private?" She gestured to the busy waiting room and for the first time, I realised we had a sizeable audience.

"Yes," I nodded, filled with shame. "I'm sorry. It's – it's been a difficult day."

"I'm aware." She led me along a wide corridor and inside a small room with a low sofa and a stained, round coffee table beside it, a pile of sticky, torn magazines stacked haphazardly on top of it. "Take a seat."

"No, thank you."

She nodded and pushed the door closed. "My name is Doctor Shaw. I'm a registrar on the surgical team. My colleague, Mr Prince, has been in theatre with your wife this afternoon."

"Theatre?"

"Yes. The damage to the artery was significant, and

warranted immediate repair. Don't worry, Mr Prince specialises in vascular surgery. Megan went straight in on arrival and I've been informed that the surgery was successful. She's in recovery now."

"Can I see her?"

She shook her head. "Not yet. Mr Taylor, are you aware of any reason to explain why your wife tried to take her own life?" I stared at her, unable to speak. She clasped her fingers together in front of her. "I've been informed that someone from the psychiatric team will be coming to assess your wife later this evening. I'm sorry to tell you that currently, Megan is very distressed. Occasionally this can happen after a general anaesthetic. But she's been awake forty-five minutes now with no signs of lucidity. And combined with the suicide attempt, I think we have a good reason to suspect an issue with her mental health."

"You think she's mad?"

"Not mad. *Ill*. And I'm not qualified to make that assessment. But I would like to hear your thoughts on her recent moods. Her behaviour."

I nodded. "She hasn't been herself. Not since..." I

broke off, shaking my head sadly. "Not since we had our second son two weeks ago. She hasn't adjusted well." Doctor Shaw nodded, waiting for me to continue. "She hasn't been herself," I repeated.

"Okay." She pursed her lips. "Well, I will pass that on. It will likely be a few hours before we'll know any more. If you would like to go home, we can give you a call when we know what's happening."

"No. I'm not leaving. I want to see her. Can't I see her now?"

She shook her head. "I'm afraid not. As I said, she's currently quite distressed."

"She's probably terrified. She's woken up in hospital surrounded by strangers, of course she's distressed!"

She flashed an empathetic smile. "I know this is difficult, Mr Taylor. Honestly, the best thing you can do for your wife is to go and rest so you can be there for her when she's able to have visitors. But if you really insist on staying, nobody will stop you. Why don't you give your mobile number to the receptionist, and pop down to the cafe for something to eat? It's open for another hour and I'm sure you've barely had chance to think of food today. We will call you as soon as your wife is fit for visitors."

I took a deep breath in through my nostrils, feeling them flare as I realised I was fighting a losing battle. "Fine," I conceded, my voice thick with barely concealed fury. "But tell her I'm here, okay? Let her know I'm right here waiting."

"I will." She opened the door, stepping out into the bright lights of the corridor, closing it behind her to give me some privacy. I sat down heavily on the worn grey sofa, my head in my hands as I let myself soak in the relief that Megan was alive. I hadn't realised how terrified I was, until she had said those words. It was torture to be so close, in the very same building as her, knowing she was struggling, scared, and yet not being permitted to go to her. I could only hope they made their assessment soon, because my patience was hanging on by a thread and I needed answers that could explain to me what was going on with my wife.

"Post what?" I asked as I hurried along the corridor behind the flailing tails of the doctor's white coat. Four painfully long hours had passed since Doctor Shaw had left me in the little room. I hadn't left the ward. I hadn't eaten. I couldn't. I'd simply paced back and forth in front of the receptionist's desk, not giving them the option of forgetting my presence. I didn't want to be off eating sandwiches when the time came to see Megan.

I'd managed a quick call to my mother, relieved that she sounded more than happy to help out by having the boys overnight and then I had watched as the clock above the desk ticked away minute after minute, hour after hour. It was gone nine p.m. when an Asian man with bushy eyebrows and silver rimmed glasses walked briskly up to me and introduced himself as Doctor Laghari.

"Postpartum Psychosis," he repeated now. "It can also be called Puerperal Psychosis."

"I've never heard of it."

"No, I don't expect you have. It's rare. Only around one in every thousand women will develop the condition, but when they do, it is serious."

"But... you can cure it?" I asked hopefully, following him onto a ward, past closed doors and curtained off bays. He paused, turning to face me.

"It can be cured, yes. But not overnight. Your wife is very unwell, Mr Taylor. And right now, it's quite clear she is a risk to both herself and her children. Often, we will place both mother and baby in a unit together during the recovery process, but unfortunately, your wife is not ready for that proximity." His glasses slid down the bridge of his nose and he pushed them back with the pad of his thumb. "We have found her a bed in a secure psychiatric unit at Maybrook Hospital, we will be transferring her tonight."

"Tonight?" I repeated, reeling at the information. "What do you mean by secure? Like a prison or something? You want to lock her up? She isn't a criminal, for god sake!"

"Nobody is making that accusation. But she needs twenty-four hour surveillance and care to keep her safe as she moves forward with her treatment."

I leaned against the wall, shaking my head. "Is it really that bad?" I asked. I'd been thinking she would get some antidepressants and have to go to a drop in group, maybe have the midwife increase her visits. But I'd never considered that they might not let her come home.

"I'm afraid so," Doctor Laghari said gravely.

"How long for?"

"I couldn't say. But it might be several months. You need to prepare yourself for that."

"Months? But, she can't be away from our children for that long. They need her! They need to be with her, especially the newborn," I insisted, remembering all the books and studies Megan had quoted from back when we'd had Toby. All the talk of early bonding and brain development and emotional security. She couldn't be apart from Milo when he was so tiny. It wasn't right.

Doctor Laghari gave a slow nod. "I understand that. And so do the doctors at the unit your wife is heading to. And you can trust me when I say that as soon as it's safe for both mother and baby, they will be transferred to a unit where they can be together. But right now, as difficult as it is, it's in their best interests to be kept apart."

He glanced at his watch. "You can see her briefly, but I should warn you, she may not recognise you. We have given her morphine for the pain and a sedative to calm her down." He didn't wait for me to respond before he pushed open the door to the room, stepping inside. I followed, uncertainly, shell-shocked at what he'd told me.

The shock was instantly replaced with anger as I looked past him. "What the hell have you done to her!" I gasped. Megan was lying on her back on a bed in the centre of the room, her arms and legs spread wide. Thick straps were buckled tightly around her ankles, across her waist, around the uninjured wrist and at the elbow on the opposite arm. Blue, padded bumpers ran around the bars on both sides of the hospital bed. "What did you do to her? You've tied her up!"

"For her own safety, and that of the staff working with her. As I said, she became quite distressed. This was communicated in violence. The restraints are padded and will be removed as soon as we can trust that Megan is calm and will not try to lash out." Two nurses on the opposite side of the room blushed, busying themselves with writing in their folders, closing the blinds for the evening.

"This is like a fucking horror movie," I breathed, staring at the bed. I walked to the side of it, looking down at the prone figure of my wife. She looked so fragile. So tiny amongst the wires and tubes that surrounded her. Her eyes were half open, unfocused as she stared up at the polystyrene tiles that made up the ceiling.

"Meg?" I said softly. "Megan, it's me. I'm here." She gave no response. I glanced over my shoulder, raising an eyebrow in question.

"She's been unresponsive since she arrived. The sedative will only make that worse I'm afraid. Do you know how long she's been having hallucinations?"

I shook my head. "Hallucinations?"

"Yes. She was experiencing quite vivid ones when I assessed her."

"I – I don't know," I admitted. "I didn't realise it was this bad."

Megan turned her head slowly in my direction and the psychiatrist stepped forward, watching closely.

"Nate?" she whispered, her voice hoarse.

"Yes. Yes, I'm here. I'm right here."

"Where's Toby?" she asked urgently. Before I could offer an answer, she let out a blood-curdling scream. "Where have you taken Toby? Bring him to me! Bring me my son!" She fought against her restraints, flailing fruitlessly against them. "I want my fucking son, now!" she screamed, her face red, her eyes empty.

"You have *two* sons, Megan," I replied acidly. My eyes stung with furious tears as anger and fear combined in my gut. I didn't want to see her like this. The memory of what she'd done to my children, of what would have happened if I'd chosen to eat lunch at my desk instead of coming home, was all I could concentrate on. The images of what I would have found after pushing my key in the lock at the end of a long day, the cold, lifeless bodies, my poor Toby locked in a house full of corpses, poisoned my mind, a madness of its very own. I willed her to pull herself together. She was still screaming, her body arching up as if she could break free of the bed. "Megan!" I yelled. "Stop this! You have two sons! Two! And you need to get a grip if you want to see them again. This isn't you!" I yelled over the wail of her voice, gripping the padded bars at the side of her bed.

"Nate." I felt a firm pressure at my elbow and turned. "Come away. She can't help it," Doctor Laghari said, guiding me back towards the door. "Your wife is ill. Reasoning with her will get you nowhere."

"I don't understand how this could have happened! This isn't her. Not at all. She's not the type to even get mood swings. She's a stable woman and she's a good mother. How could this just happen out of the blue? How can she just change like this? She's abandoned our children and she's not even *trying* to see sense!" I yelled, willing her to hear me. To argue. *Anything,* so long as I knew she was there. That *my* Megan hadn't just disappeared and left me to deal with the consequences.

"I know it's difficult," the doctor replied, leading me expertly out of the room, flashing the nurses a look as he pulled the door closed. "You're in for a tough time over the coming weeks. But for now, the best thing you can do is to go home to your children and get some rest. You won't reach her tonight." He patted me on the shoulder and turned away. I watched him leave, bracing myself against the wall to stop my legs from giving out, then pulled my phone from my pocket. On the first ring, she answered.

"Nate, is that you?"

"Mum," I said thickly. "Meg's being sectioned."

Chapter Twenty-Four

Megan

I wished that I could believe that I was in some hellish kind of afterlife, that I was dead and none of these awful things were really happening to me, but I knew I was very much alive. The pain where I'd cut my wrist throbbed unbearably, almost distracting enough to switch off the constant blanket of fear. But not quite.

My memories were fuzzy. I remembered cutting my wrist myself, but I couldn't recall why I'd done it, not when I had promised to protect Toby from Milo. And where was he now? How could I be of any use, strapped to a bed in this bare, sterile room?

There was a constant stream of people, strangers coming in and out, talking over my head, touching me, tugging at the straps and tubes that covered my body. None of them would listen. Nobody seemed to realise the danger we were all in. It had taken hours before I'd realised the truth. And it was clever. *Of course it was.* Because who would suspect a doctor? A nurse? Who wouldn't give them their trust? It was the perfect cover. But I'd seen their empty, black eyes. Their knowing smiles. They were with *him*. Milo. Under his command.

I fought hard against my restraints, breathless as I tried to get free. I could feel the pull and rip as my stitches reopened, the pain shooting up my arm, but I couldn't let it prevent me from getting out. Getting home.

My head span and I realised I'd been drugged again. "This should help," a bodiless voice echoed above me. I shook my head, unable to focus on the nurse's hovering face.

"You," I whispered. "You need to help. You... don't understand... danger... we're in danger," I murmured, feeling my body grow heavy, my eyelids closing against my will.

There were voices coming from nearby. Arguing. I dragged myself to consciousness, feeling as though I'd slept for far too long.

"See, she's awake. I'm not disturbing her."

"Mr Taylor – "

"It's Nate. And I've heard you out. But I want to see my wife and I'm not leaving until you let me."

There was an exasperated sigh. "Ten minutes."

I heard the door open and close and then footsteps approaching my bed. *Nate had come! He would help me. He would rescue me from these monsters, their mind controlling drugs.* I struggled to sit up but the restraints pinned me to my back.

"Meg?" he said cautiously.

"Nate, thank god! You have to help me. You have to undo these straps. Quickly, before they come back!"

He shook his head sadly and I stared up at him in confusion. "Nate, there isn't much time!" I whispered urgently. I glanced behind him, my stomach instantly tightening at the empty space. "Nate," I said, my voice chilling even to my own ears. I didn't dare to believe that he could have been so stupid. "Where is Toby? Where's Milo? Tell me you have them here, with *you?* Nate, tell me you haven't left them!"

He gave a slow shake of his head. "I'm glad you

bothered to ask after *both* of them this time," he spat with uncharacteristic venom.

My eyes widened. "Nate!"

"I'm sorry." He rubbed his eyes. "God, I'm really sorry. That was uncalled for. I know you can't help it, but this is hard, Megan, really fucking hard. I don't know what to do. How to make this better. I just want my life back. I want *you* back, Meg, but you're not there, are you?"

His words ran around me, empty and meaningless. I couldn't focus on them. All I knew was that my children were not safe. Not at all. "Nate!" I demanded, my mind spinning with terror. "Where are my children? Tell me where they are!" I yelled, no longer bothering to keep my voice down so we could escape unnoticed.

"They're fine, Megan," he said, his voice still cold. "They are with my mother."

"No!" I gasped. "No!"

"What – "

"It's not safe! You can't trust her, Nate! Don't trust her! You have to go. Go and get them right now.

Don't you get it? She wants to take them from me. She's planned this from the start, I know she has! You are the only person I can trust. Please, Nate, go and get them. You have to bring them to me. Do you understand?"

"She's my *mother*, Meg. She loves them as much as we do. She's not going to hurt them for Christ sake!" I could see the crease between his eyebrows, the hardness in his features. There was no love in his eyes anymore. Jane had got to him too. She was beneath his skin. Chipping away at him, bringing him onside. The fear was overwhelming, the realisation that only *I* could save them now. Nobody else was going to help me. I thrashed hard against my bonds, determined to break free, to get my children back where I could watch over them.

"I want my children!" I screamed. "Bring me my fucking children! I want them now!"

The door burst open and two male nurses ran at me, a needle glinting in the light. "No!" I bellowed, my lungs bursting, my throat raw. "Don't you dare touch me! Nate! Nate, stop them! Help me, Nate!

Don't let them touch me!"

I felt the sharp stab as the needle broke through my skin, Nate's face looming above me, tears dripping down his stubble coated cheeks. It felt so real. But Nate wouldn't cry in a room full of people. He was so private. So controlled. *It can't be happening... none of this can be happening. It's not real...* The edges of my vision darkened, my ears ringing with voices I couldn't separate from one another. And I knew. It *couldn't* have been my Nate. Because he would never let this happen to me. He would have helped. My Nate would have saved me.

Chapter Twenty-Five

Jane

"Now, let's find you your storybook, shall we darling?" I said, leading Toby upstairs into Nate's old bedroom. I wasn't one of those mothers who kept their child's room as some sort of shrine long after they'd left home. You could always feel it in those houses. The emptiness. The ghosts of memories that were all those women had left. It made their homes stagnant and eerie.

Of course, it was never easy to move forward. Not when you would prefer to stay put exactly where you were, at a time when love was abundant and you never doubted that you were needed. Valuable to someone else. Life with young children was like that. You never had a chance to question your purpose. It was evident in everything you did.

But you couldn't stay in the past. It was impossible to preserve the love that had passed. You couldn't bottle old memories and survive on those alone. You had to make new ones. Adapt and change so you didn't get left behind.

Nate's old single bed had long since been sold on, as had his little pine wardrobe where his corduroy dungarees and soft flannel pyjamas had once lived. A few treasured items were stored in a drawstring linen bag in my dressing table, but the rest had been passed on as he outgrew them. What I *had* kept, however, were his toys. And with them, I had created an enviable playroom. A room that meant that Toby was only too happy to spend the day at my house. That if too much time passed without a visit to grandma, he would request one himself. It was my secret weapon for ensuring they didn't forget about me and I loved how happy it made Toby. I knew Milo would love it too as he got older.

We pushed inside the large room, decorated in soft cream paper with blue and green bunting strung around the walls. Toby ran straight to the little wooden kitchen, pulling out stainless steel pans, frying a felt egg to feed to the collection of rag-dolls that sat, watching with beady glass eyes from the child sized rocking chair beside him. When Nate had been small, he'd given each of them names. Jasper, Flossy and Jim. Toby had come up with his own names for them and I encouraged him to put his own stamp on things. I wanted him to feel at home. Free to make changes. To know that Grandma's house was a place where he could always feel safe and loved.

I carried Milo in the crook of my arm past the wooden garage and box of cars, the polka-dot teepee and the teddy bears picnic, and squatted down beside the well stocked bookshelves, searching through them quickly. I kept them organised by size and theme, and alphabetically within those sections, knowing I'd never have to see the disappointment on my grandchildren's faces when I couldn't find the book they really wanted.

Sliding a yellow spined picture book from the shelf, I smiled, then bit my lip reflexively at the guilt that swelled within me. I couldn't help but think of Megan, wondering how she was coping, if she was aware of what was happening to her. It felt wrong to be enjoying my time with her children so much, whilst she was suffering, scared and confused far across town.

I couldn't pretend I didn't feel guilty for not doing more. I'd known she wasn't right. And yet I'd let myself be cowed by her. Pushed out, until things had escalated dangerously out of control. I could have done more.

I kissed Milo, holding him closer, relieved to know that no harm could come to him now. I would take care of them both. And Nate too. Heaven knew he needed looking after, after what he'd been through recently. He needed me and I was only too happy to be there for him. I stood up, smiling across the room at Toby.

"Here's your book, sweetheart. How about we go and get Milo a nice bottle of milk, then we can snuggle up and read it together on the sofa?"

He nodded, grabbing one of the rag-dolls, the one he called Phoenix, before following me out to the landing. "And after that, you can do some more cooking with me in the big kitchen. We need to get daddy's dinner ready before he comes home, don't we?"

"And Mama?" he asked.

"Not today," I said, kissing his soft, warm cheek. "But never mind. We'll manage on our own, won't we?" I walked carefully beside him as he bumped down the stairs on his bottom, Milo's sweet baby breath on my neck, and despite myself I felt lucky to have them with me, bringing life to the house again in that special way only children can.

Chapter Twenty-Six

Nate

"Mum!" I called, pushing my feet into my shoes. "Are you sure you don't mind? You won't lose your job?" I heard brisk footsteps as she walked from the kitchen, entering the living room with Milo in her arms, Toby hot on her heels. He had clung to his grandma the past few days, like a lifeboat in a shipwreck. He couldn't bear to be parted from her, and I knew she'd been letting him sleep in her bed.

It was good for them to be here, away from the vivid memories of what had happened at our own house. I'd been sleeping on the lumpy sofa in mum's living room rather than go back to face that place. I didn't know if it would ever feel like home again, if I would ever look at it and not see the lifeless body of my wife being carried out on a stretcher, that copper smear of blood from where I'd brushed my hand against the wallpaper, a permanent reminder of what she'd done. I loved the comfort of being back at my childhood home. I felt safe here and I knew Toby did too.

Mum pushed a duster into the wide pocket on the front of her apron and I smiled, taking in her bright red, floral patterned fifties style dress, that swishing skirt that always reminded me of being small, hiding in the folds of it whenever I felt uneasy.

Her brown hair was tied up in a loose bun and she looked warm and homey in the well worn apron she always donned for housework. She had a second one that was strictly for cooking. "Nate, darling," she smiled now. "I have leave. I told you. And I can't think of a better use for it than doing this." She sat down in the wide, velvet upholstered armchair, adjusting Milo into an upright position so that he could look over her shoulder at the fish tank against the wall. The bright tropical fish darted back and forth and he stared, uncomprehending, his eyes following them across the water. "You know you don't even need to ask," she continued. "But what about *your* work, darling? Have you spoken to them?"

I nodded. It hadn't been easy summoning the courage to call my boss, not because I didn't think he would be understanding – I already knew he would. But I'd put it off because I was embarrassed. I still didn't fully understand what was happening to my wife, but it felt shameful to admit that she was currently locked up, spouting nonsense, completely unreachable despite being there in body. I didn't want to admit that my wife, my beautiful, playful, warm, funny wife had been replaced with this paranoid, unreasonable lunatic who had tried to kill herself and risked our sons' lives in the process. It still felt impossible to me that any of this could be happening. A living nightmare. I was grateful that my boss hadn't pushed me to talk about it in detail, because I knew I wouldn't have made it through that conversation without falling apart.

I scratched my chin, watching Toby as he played on the carpet, running his trains back and forth along the little wooden track that had once belonged to me. "He signed off two weeks compassionate leave. It's a good company, thankfully. But I'll have to go back after that. Even if I *could* have more time, it would be unpaid. I just can't afford to do that. We'll lose the house." I looked up at her, my head throbbing. Rubbing my temples, I sighed, weary with the whole situation. "They said it could be months, Mum. *Months*. I have no idea how we're going to cope. What I'm going do with the boys."

"I've been thinking about that," she said, pursing her lips. "What they both need right now is stability. I'm not going to see you put them in some nursery where they'll have to fight for attention, and besides, I doubt you would even find one that would accept Milo at his age. He's far too young."

"I'll advertise for a nanny."

"No." She shook her head vehemently. "You'll do no such thing. I've been quite happy pottering away at my little part-time job at the garden centre up until now, but I'm not going to spend my days sweeping floors and watering seedlings when I have something far more meaningful I could be doing. I'm retiring, Nate. I'm going to take care of my grandchildren, and I'll have no arguments."

"Mum, I won't let you quit your job for me. I'll figure something out."

"I've already put my notice in. It's done."

I stared at her, shocked, yet absurdly happy to realise that my sons would be taken care of. It felt like a massive weight had been lifted from my shoulders. I knew I could trust her to take care of them as if they were her own. I felt the prick of tears in my eyes and swallowed thickly. "I can't thank you enough for doing that, Mum. I really can't."

"I don't want you to thank me. It's what family is for. And I think it's best if the three of you continue to stay here with me... until Megan is able to come home."

I nodded. "But... what will you do when that happens?" I asked, suddenly remembering how resistant Megan had always been – even before Milo – about mum getting too involved in the children's upbringing. She wouldn't like it. She'd feel suffocated.

Mum gave a casual shrug. "That could be a long way off. We'll figure it out when it happens."

I chewed my lip, knowing we should come up with a long term plan now, yet not wanting to upset her or change her mind about helping me. "Okay," I said finally. "If you're sure?"

"I couldn't be more sure," she grinned, kissing Milo's cheek.

"I'm going to pop over there now then. See how she's getting on. You'll be okay?"

"Of course." She stood up. "Just let me just get you a sandwich to take with you. You're not eating properly."

"Mum, you don't have to – " I started, but she was already out the door. Not more than a few seconds passed before Toby put down his train and followed her into the kitchen. I watched him go with a deep sense of sadness, knowing that despite his young age, the events of the past few weeks would have affected him profoundly. I just hoped he wasn't too traumatised by what his mother had done to him and his brother.

Seeing those bruises on his arm had shocked me to my core. I had never in a million years believed Megan could hurt him, and though I knew it wasn't intentional, I still couldn't help but hate her on some level for it. I hoped that Toby would be able to forgive her. That he wouldn't fear her when she came home. I hoped I wouldn't either, but I wasn't sure I would ever be able to walk out of the house and leave her in sole charge of my sons without fearing for what I would find when I returned. My phone rang and I grabbed it from the table, not recognising the number on the screen.

"Hello?"

"Mr Taylor?"

"Yes. Who is this?"

"My name is Doctor Parkins. I'm your wife's psychiatric consultant."

"Oh, right. Is she okay?"

"She is very much the same as she was on admission. That is the reason for my call. I've started her on a course of treatment – anti-psychotics, mood stabilisers, which should begin to take effect in the coming days. We'll see how she reacts and adjust her dose accordingly."

"Right."

"But I'm afraid, in the meantime, I would prefer if you didn't visit. Megan is still very confused and disorientated. She believes her children have been kidnapped and she is reacting very violently – "

"What if I brought them in to visit? You know, to show her they're okay – "

"No. Absolutely not. It would be upsetting for them and given her current condition, it wouldn't be safe. And honestly, it wouldn't help. She's not at a stage where reason and logic will have any effect. Sadly, it's not as simple as just showing her they're okay. She's not in a position to realise that she's unwell yet. She is lost in the grip of her delusions. What she needs right now is medication, supervision and therapy. Now, all things being well, it shouldn't be too long before you're able to visit, but I don't think it would be helpful at this stage."

"I don't want to just leave her there!" I said, unable to stop myself from picturing how scared and small she'd looked strapped to the hospital bed when I last saw her.

"I know. But the state she's in right now, you would be doing her a favour. Seeing you would only confuse her more. I can promise you, she is getting the care she needs and we will support her through this. She has someone with her around the clock."

I gripped the phone, realising with a wave of fresh guilt that I was relieved to be absolved of my duty. I didn't *want* to visit when she was so terrifyingly absent. Lost. I didn't need any more material for my nightmares, I had enough to last for years as it was. But I would have gone. Despite everything, my anger towards her, my discomfort, I would have gone. Because she deserved it. And I knew that if she were well and our roles were reversed, she would be there for me.

"Okay," I agreed, quietly. "But I'm going to keep calling. I want to be told everything, okay? Any changes, you contact me immediately."

"Of course."

I ended the call, holding the phone between my palms, squeezing it tightly. A sudden memory came to mind, the day I'd asked Megan to marry me. We'd been camping in the New Forest and though I'd planned to make it romantic, everything that could possibly go wrong, had.

First the pub I'd booked for the all important dinner had shut because of a burst water pipe and Megan had been so hungry that we'd ended up having a row over where to go instead. We had driven three miles to another restaurant, only to be told they were fully booked, and then got lost driving around trying to find what Trip Advisor described as "a little gem of a country pub" though we never found the place to make up our own minds about that.

In the end, we'd bought a disposable BBQ and a pack of sausages from a village shop and headed back to the campsite, trying to make the best of a bad situation. I'd plied Megan with wine, got the sausages on to cook and things had been on the up, when one of the wild horses had come over to investigate. Meg had fished around in the bag of groceries and pulled out an apple to offer to the horse. Seconds later, she'd screamed, dropping her wine on the grass. The bloody thing had bitten her fingers.

We'd spent the next thirty minutes in reception, while the moody owner searched high and low for the first aid kit, eventually coming back with a dusty, grime covered box filled with out of date bandages and alcohol gel. By the time we made it back to the tent, the sausages were burned and fat drops of rain had begun to fall. It had been as far from romantic as you could get and I'd jacked in the whole idea of proposing, deciding to start afresh on another, hopefully more fortuitous, day.

But then, as we'd snuggled down in our double sleeping bag, listening to the sounds of the rain falling against the canvas, Meg had moved into my arms and in the pitch black, we'd made love. Afterwards, with the rain subsiding, I'd unzipped the front of the tent so we could look up at the stars and with her nestled in my arms, I'd proposed. It had seemed like the most natural thing in the world. No orchestrated romance. No bells and whistles. Just me and the woman I adored, tiny in our little space in the wide open universe. She'd smiled up at me, a knowing look in her eyes, and accepted.

It seemed like another life now. Like looking back on people who you'd fallen out of touch with. People I missed. And *fuck*, I missed her. I wanted *my* Megan back. *My* life. *My* home. I didn't want to be feeling like this lost little boy who had to lean on his mummy to get through each day.

I looked up as she bustled back into the room with a Tupperware box filled with sandwiches, stopping in her tracks as she caught sight of me. "Oh, Nate!" she exclaimed, rushing over, putting her arms around me. "Oh, sweetheart!"

"I just want it to be over, Mum. I want her to come back to me."

"I know you do, darling. And she *will*. You just need to be patient."

"I don't know how much more of this I can take."

She pulled back, looking me in the eye. "You *will* get through this. I know it doesn't seem like it right now, but it will get better for you." She squeezed my shoulder. "And in the meantime, I'm going to take care of all of you," she smiled. "You always have me."

Chapter Twenty-Seven

Megan

Six days later

I pulled myself up in bed and scratched at the dressing that covered my wrist, the stitches and scabs frustratingly itchy. The sounds of the nurses coming up and down the hall doing the rounds with the meds had quickly become familiar to me. It meant that the doctors would follow shortly afterwards, and after that, someone would bring me breakfast. I still wasn't allowed to go out into the communal dining room, but I no longer had to have a nurse in with me at all times, nor did I have to be strapped down. It was hard to believe it had come to that.

I took a sip from the plastic cup of water on my side table, cradling it between my palms. My memories of the first few days in this place were colourful, frightening and confused. Although I could now reason with myself about the truth – that not all of it had been real and that I'd been hallucinating and delusional, I still shuddered at those memories. The visions filled with blood and demons, fears over protecting my children and yet terror over what Milo was capable of.

I squeezed my eyes tightly shut now, not wanting to think about it, hoping that the nurse would arrive with my medication soon. I hadn't asked questions about what they were giving me. At first I hadn't even been aware, and after that, it hadn't seemed to matter. I had wanted to die anyway so there was no fear on my part when it came to the toxic drugs they were pumping into my body. But I could feel that they were working. Winning the battle against whatever it was that had made my mind break in the first place. I felt more like myself than I had since giving birth. And I wasn't sure that was a good thing. With sanity came reflection. Guilt. Fear for what lay ahead.

Nate hadn't come. They told me that he'd been there, at the hospital at the beginning. But he hadn't been to see me for days. Maybe longer. I wasn't sure I blamed him. He probably couldn't even bring himself to look at me after what I'd put him through.

There was a knock at the door and it opened, Doctor Parkins entering with measured steps. I'd grown used to his cautious manner now, after initially finding him aloof and distant. It had taken a little while for me to realise that he was simply assessing the mood, not wanting to push his own thoughts and feelings onto me.

He looked at me now, his arms folded over his thick knitted sweater. He was tall and robust looking, a simple gold wedding band on his sun-browned hand, his grey hair surprisingly thick for his age which I guessed to be at least sixty. He had a presence about him that made me feel instantly safe. Confident and assertive, yet calm and empathetic. A born doctor, I thought.

"Good morning, Megan," he said quietly.

"Hi."

"How are you? Did you sleep?"

I nodded. "I did. I had nightmares," I admitted.

He nodded and took a seat by the window. "And when you woke? Were you still in the nightmare?"

I raised an eyebrow. "This whole situation is a

nightmare, isn't it? I've lost my mind, my husband and my babies."

He pursed his lips, waiting silently.

"But I know that isn't what you mean, is it?"

"No."

I sighed. "When I woke, I knew where I was and what had happened. I didn't see anything that shouldn't be here," I shrugged.

"On a scale of one to ten, one being not at all, ten being extreme terror, where would you put your fear levels at?"

"I don't know."

"There's no right or wrong answer, Megan."

I looked at his kind expression and shook my head. "I'm scared I've lost them," I whispered, hearing my voice crack. "I'm scared they won't forgive me. That Nate won't love me anymore and Toby will be scared of me. And I'm scared that social services won't let me be their mother now, because I don't deserve them after what I did. How crazy is that? After all my delusions that someone was trying to steal them from me, my own mother-in-law even, after all that turns out to be a figment of my imagination, I could lose them anyway because I'm not fit to be their mother." I shook my head. "I'm scared, Doctor Parkins. But I'm not afraid that my newborn is hatching an evil master-plan to kill his brother anymore. Does that answer your question?" I said with a wry smile.

"I think it does, Megan," he nodded. "Your fears are quite normal. You've been through a huge amount in such a short space of time, but you are doing so well. I'm very pleased with your progress so far, and it's clear to me that you are responding well to the current treatment plan. Yours are the fears of a sane woman right now. The nurses tell me they've had no issues and you've been cooperative in your care for the past forty-eight hours. This is very good, Megan. It doesn't always happen so fast."

"But I don't feel like *me* yet. I feel so sad. So very broken."

He scratched his chin, regarding me with questioning eyes. "A period of depression following treatment for Postpartum Psychosis is to be expected,

I'm afraid. Your mind has been on an absolute rollercoaster of emotions and experiences, and the comedown is hard. It's normal to feel sad, depressed even, for a while. It will take time to process all that has happened and move on. I do have an idea which might help, though."

"What is it?"

He leaned forward, resting an elbow on his knee, his chin cupped casually in his palm, though I had a horrible feeling I wasn't going to like what he had to say.

"I believe we are ready to move on to the next stage. Ideally, I would like to transfer you across to our mother and baby unit, where you can keep Milo with you, under close supervision. It's always our preference not to separate mother and baby if at all avoidable. This is an important time for your bonding. I'd like to invite your husband to bring your children in to visit tomorrow, and all being well, we can make arrangements for the transfer. How do you feel about that, Megan?"

"I don't think I'm ready," I said, shaking my head.

"I don't want to see him."

"Who? Your husband?"

"No," I replied, crying now. I couldn't seem to stem the flow of emotions that his words had triggered within me. "The baby," I said softly.

"Milo. His name is Milo. Use it, Megan."

"I don't want to see him... not yet."

"What are you afraid of?" he asked, though I was sure he already knew. I was terrified of being near him. I couldn't be certain that seeing him wouldn't set everything off again. Send me spiralling into that awful place I'd only just clawed my way out of. And, I was scared that despite the knowledge I now carried, the diagnosis that was supposed to make sense of everything, I was afraid that I still wouldn't love him. That I'd look at him and feel nothing. Or worse.

"I don't think I can do it," I said simply. I couldn't bring myself to voice the rest.

Doctor Parkins nodded and rose to his feet. "Okay. I'll give you a little more time. But you will have to step out of your comfort zone and move forward soon, Megan. I want you to spend your therapy session today looking at these fears, and trying to find a way you can move past them. Try and be as open as you can with Doctor Sandringham. It will help."

I nodded, ashamed of myself. "I feel like I'm letting everyone down. I hate myself for it," I said as he made for the door.

He turned, flashing me a warm smile. "They love you. And they understand."

"Can – can you ask Nate to visit me? Just by himself?"

"I'll do that." There was a tap at the door behind him and the nurse entered.

"Morning, love. I've got your meds for you. Doctor," she nodded.

"Good morning," he replied. "I would like Mrs Taylor to have her meals in the day room from now on," he instructed, throwing me a wink.

My stomach flipped at the idea of it, but he was gone before I could put up at fight. He was clearly not going to let me get comfortable, and I liked him all the more for his tenacity. I just wished I could have a few more weeks hiding in my room before I had to face the rest of the world.

Chapter Twenty-Eight

Megan

It was like being back at school again, an experience I could quite happily have gone my whole life without reliving. The nurse handed me a cup of tepid tea in a red plastic mug, her eyes meeting mine briefly, questioning. She'd waited with me as I'd dressed, then walked me to the day-room, keeping up a stream of small talk in what I could only assume was her pointless attempt to make me feel comfortable.

I gave an unsteady nod as I took the cup from her outstretched hands, and let my eyes wander around the large room, assessing the scene. I'd expected a long, bare table with cheap plastic chairs, the kind you get in schools. I'd pictured it to be like a scene from Oliver Twist, only instead of workhouse orphans, the table would be crammed with dribbling, screaming or blank eyed patients who would frighten the life out of me.

Instead, I was amazed to find myself in a bright,

comfortable looking room dotted with round tables, four chairs at each of them, wide sofas beneath the windows and piles of books and boardgames lining the shelves.

It felt very casual, not at all like they had all been waiting for the new arrivals to pounce on. Nobody made me stand at the front of the room and introduce myself and only a couple of people even bothered to look up to scrutinise me over their breakfast. A few of the patients were playing chess and backgammon around the tables, and others had taken plates of toast off to eat in a quiet spot by themselves. At first glance, it all seemed very normal, but when I looked closer, I began to spot the signs of madness amongst the people around me.

A woman dressed in a worn pair of flannel pj's, her feet bare, was muttering a quiet but constant stream of words under her breath, her gaze fixed on the tabletop. Another woman with short, dark hair that looked as though she'd hacked it off herself, walked repeatedly to the exit, trying the locked door handle, before being directed back to her seat. The nurse would guide her across the room, waiting beside her as she lowered herself into the chair, and no sooner had the nurse walked away, the dark haired woman would rise to her feet, walking right back to the door to repeat the whole process again. I watched in fascination, wondering if my ability to see the madness in their actions was a sign that I was no longer in the grip of it myself.

I wished I could feel some sort of relief in that, rather than the persistent numbness that hovered like a permanent black cloud over my head. It was hard to imagine I would ever find my way back to the person I'd been before.

That Megan hadn't known the things *I* knew. She hadn't experienced pain, darkness, despair, to the degrees I now understood. I'd been changed by my experiences, and despite the fact that Doctor Parkins and my therapist both told me that I would come out of this a stronger person, I couldn't bring myself to believe them. It was easy for them to give advice based on their studies, their fancy degrees. They hadn't *lived* this. They didn't really know. I had been happy, before all of this. I'd loved my life. But that was gone. Now I was just existing. Nothing more. Reduced to a jumbled mess of guilt, bitterness, blame, and a persistent hollow feeling inside my chest that might never be filled again.

"Hello!" a voice called cheerfully. I glanced over, seeing a young, spiky haired woman with thick rimmed glasses and a smattering of freckles on her pale face. She was smiling at me, waving like we were old friends as she pointed to the seat beside her. I shook my head, turning away from her.

I wasn't here to make friends. This wasn't a bloody holiday, I didn't deserve distraction, nor conversation, even if it only amounted to weird small talk with a total stranger. I walked to the far side of the room, choosing a hard backed chair that faced the window, noticing that it was bolted to the floor. A quick glance behind me confirmed that the same was true for the other chairs. The tables too. *I guess we can't be trusted not to throw the furniture,* I thought, pursing my lips. I took a sip of my tea, the plasticy taste of the cup permeating the lukewarm, overly milky drink. With a grimace, I put it down on the table, freezing as I saw the person approaching me.

"Hi."

"You came," I breathed, looking up at the dishevelled figure of my husband. He had dark circles under his eyes and wore a cautious expression. "I didn't think Doctor Parkins would get in touch so quickly."

"I called him." He sat down opposite me. "I've called every day. He said you were feeling a bit better. Are you?" His eyes pleaded with me, desperate for some good news.

I shrugged. "I don't know if better is the right word," I admitted. "I feel awful. But I think my grip on reality has improved. I don't think my baby is trying to take over the world," I said, trying to sound jokey but hearing the way my voice broke. It wasn't funny. Not now, and I doubted it ever would be. "Nate, I'm so sorry," I whispered, the tears, always so close to the surface now, already beginning to fall. I couldn't seem to rein in my emotions anymore. "I'm so sorry for what I put you through."

He watched me, his expression hard and unreadable and I wondered if I'd been right. That what we'd had was broken beyond repair. He would never be able to find the strength to forgive me for what I'd done. I couldn't blame him. But then as the hollowness swelled inside my chest and I considered running back to my room to hide, he dropped to his knees in front of me, pulling me from my chair into his arms. "I missed you so much," he said, his lips on my hair. "I thought... I thought I was too late, Meg. I thought I'd lost you."

"I'm sorry," I cried, wrapping my arms tightly around his waist, my tears soaking into his shirt, not caring who might be watching. "I don't know how you can ever forgive me, Nate. I've messed everything up, I know I have. I can't believe the things I did. The awful things I thought. I'm sorry. I'm sorry, I am so fucking sorry," I sobbed. "You have to believe me!"

"I do. Shush, darling, I know you weren't thinking straight." He held me tighter, and I breathed in the smell of him, familiar and safe. I took a juddering breath, wiping my eyes on the sleeve of my jumper. "I love you," he said softly.

I looked up at him, shocked. "After all this?"

"Yes."

"I love you, too," I replied softly. He rubbed his thumb in circles over my spine, just as he had a thousand times before. "So, where do we go from here?" I asked. "I don't know how to get back to what we had."

He sighed into my hair. "We just have to try. One day at a time. It's worth fighting for, isn't it? The life we had?"

I nodded. "Yes. It is."

"And the worst part is over. We know what we're dealing with now." He bent his head lower to kiss me and for the first time since I'd arrived, I felt something close to hope.

Chapter Twenty-Nine

Megan

Five days later

"Knock knock!"

I looked up from my spot by the window in my room to see Doctor Parkins enter, a smile on his face.

"Hi," I nodded. "Good morning?"

"Busy. Just how I like it." He took a seat, his eyes on mine. "How are you?"

I took a deep breath in through my nose. "Honestly? I'm terrified. But I know we need to do this. It's like ripping off a plaster, right?"

He grinned. "Something like that."

"So, what happens next? I mean, if it goes okay?"

"You will be moved to the mother and baby unit with Milo and continue your treatment there."

I sighed. "It will feel like starting from scratch. A new doctor. New therapist."

"Oh, no, you'll still have me and Doctor Sandringham," he grinned. "I thought they'd explained. It's literally down the hall, five minutes walk, max. You won't get rid of us that easily," he chuckled.

"Oh," I said, the relief causing me to break into a rare smile. "I'm glad. Even the smallest changes feel monumental right now. So... when do we do this? I mean, do you know when – "

"They just arrived. They're in the waiting room now."

"Oh." I felt my body coil in on itself, my shoulders hunching forward as I wrung my hands together in my lap.

"You can do this, Megan. We're going to take it nice and slow. I know you're far more apprehensive over seeing Milo than you are Toby, so we're going to get your husband to come here with Milo first so you can see him without the distraction of an excitable toddler. Toby will wait with your mother-in-law, and then we'll bring him in when you're ready. How do you feel about that?"

"I just want to get it done," I admitted. "It's hard to think of Toby being here, I mean, he's in the same building as me and I didn't even know. It's weird." It was as if my mothering instincts had been dulled. I was no longer in tune with his every movement. His subtle changes in mood. I wondered if I would even know what he needed when he cried now, if I still had that instinct that had been a part of me for so long, the ability to know if he were hungry or tired or hurt, just from the pitch of his cry.

"I miss him. So much it physically hurts," I said, my hands clasping at my belly, remembering how it had felt to have him grow and wriggle inside me. "I just hope he wants to see me as much as I want to see him."

"I'm certain he does. But let's see to Milo first. Wait here, I'll be right back." I offered a silent nod and he walked briskly from the room, leaving the door wide open. I stared at it, gripping the armrests of the chair, my fingernails pressing into the soft wood. I felt edgy and afraid. What would I do? What would happen if nothing had changed? If I looked at him and felt like I had the last time I'd seen him? If I admitted it, there was no doubt that I'd be forced to stay here. They would keep me locked up for months, shut in limbo, prevented from returning to my real life.

But if I lied, if I told them what I knew they wanted to hear, I knew what would happen. I would hurt them. Toby and Milo. Or myself. Eventually, I would lose control of the charade, and it would end in a tragedy that couldn't be undone. I would put everyone at risk. I wouldn't do it. I would *not* go back to living that way.

No matter what happened, what I felt in the next few hours, I knew I had to be honest about it. I would tell Doctor Parkins and Doctor Sandringham every single thing that I was feeling, even if it meant staying here for months. For ever, even. Because my children deserved a safe place to live, they deserved security, not fear, and if that meant I couldn't be with them, I would make that sacrifice. I was at least a decent enough mother that I could do that. I could find the strength to let them go if it was going to save them.

I heard measured footsteps approaching my door and stiffened. Doctor Parkins came in to the room, smiling, Nate following behind. My gaze shot to the bundle in his arms, wrapped in a thin cotton blanket. Nate stopped near the bed, his eyes travelling over me, assessing. Cautious.

"Hi," he said. I saw the way his arm moved protectively over the baby. He didn't trust me. Doctor Parkins moved an empty chair beside me, gesturing for Nate to sit. He gave a resigned nod and moved slowly across the room. I couldn't take my eyes from the baby. Milo. A tiny, bare foot poked out from between the folds of the blanket and I swallowed back bile, remembering the day I'd stood at an open window with the intention of dropping him to the concrete two floors below. I had come so very close to the place of no return.

The chair squeaked as Nate lowered his long limbs into it and he glanced at me, then up to the Doctor. Doctor Parkins gave an encouraging nod. "That's right. Now, if you could turn so that Megan can look at Milo's face. Yes, like that," he instructed as Nate cradled Milo in a different position. I forced myself to keep watching as he moved his large hand aside and Milo's small, round face came into view. I bit my lip, noting how dry my mouth was, then swallowed, a lump forming in my throat. Dark, chocolaty brown eyes peered up at me from a chubby cheeked face. A *beautiful* face, I realised. I continued to stare, waiting for the onslaught of terror, the feelings of being buried alive by darkness to come, but it didn't happen.

I reached out, and Nate instinctively pulled back, shielding him from me. Doctor Parkins placed a firm, reassuring hand on his shoulder and gave a tiny shake of his head. With obvious reluctance, Nate turned again so I could touch the baby. I ran my fingers over the back of his chubby hand, up the sleeve of his soft, cotton vest, across his peachy smooth cheek. I let my fingers run through the soft, fluffy hair on his head, then slid my index finger into his outstretched palm, smiling as he gripped hold of it and brought it to his mouth. I looked up, tears blurring my vision as I met Nate's questioning gaze.

"Can – can I hold him?" I asked.

"I'm not – " Nate began.

"Yes," Doctor Parkins interrupted. "Nate," he said

with a nod.

"Are you sure?" Nate asked me.

"Yes. I won't hurt him. I promise, I won't," I said, meaning it. Nate sighed, then leaned forward, placing Milo in my arms. His hand continued to rest on Milo's stomach, prepared to move quickly if I should suddenly snap. But I wouldn't. I knew I wouldn't. I looked down at the sweet baby in my arms – my baby – and felt like I would burst with love for him. I knew without a flicker of doubt that he had nothing to fear from me now. I would do anything to keep him safe. Anything to protect him. I loved him. I loved him so much I could hardly believe I'd ever doubted it.

"Oh, my sweet baby," I whispered, tears flowing from my eyes, dripping in a constant stream from my chin to his blanket. "Oh, my boy. My darling boy. I'm so sorry. I'm so sorry," I cried. "What did I do? Oh my god, Milo, what did I do?" I sobbed.

"Hey, it's okay," Nate murmured, sliding an arm around my shoulder. "He's okay." He kissed my forehead, wiping my damp cheek with his thumb.

"He's perfect," I said, looking up to see Doctor

Parkins watching me. "He's so completely perfect. How could I have ever thought there was anything bad about him? God, I love him. I really do."

Nate broke into a wide smile. "So do I. We did well, Meg. Two beautiful boys." I felt his hand slide away from Milo and realised I was now holding him all by myself. No safety net. The fact that he trusted me enough to do that meant more than I could put into words.

"Thank you," I said softly, my eyes meeting his, a thousand unspoken words, apologies, promises running between us. Milo kicked his legs and I lifted his face to mine, resting my forehead against his. All I could feel was love. Immense, all consuming, unconditional love. "I will never let you down again," I whispered. He leaned forward, his tiny mouth latching onto my nose and I laughed, a sound I'd forgotten I could even make. "I think he's hungry," I grinned.

"And I think you're just the person to fix that for him," Doctor Parkins smiled. "So, how about it, Megan? Shall I make arrangements to transfer you to the mother and baby unit?"

I looked down at my son and smiled. I'd been given a second chance and I wasn't going to waste it. "Yes," I nodded. "I'm ready."

Chapter Thirty

Megan

Four weeks later

Nate unzipped the brown, leather holdall and dropped it on the narrow bed, walking around the hospital room that had been my home for almost a month now and picking up my belongings. He dropped clothes and toiletries in haphazardly, clearly in a rush to be leaving this place. Jane wasn't having that though. With a wry smile and a roll of her eyes, she reached into the bag, pulling out items of clothing, folding them properly before placing them back in a far more orderly fashion.

Toby had gone off to paint with one of the play specialists, a man called Mikey who he'd grown close to during the past month. It had been wonderful to be able to see him every day, though it was always hard to say goodbye when it was time for him to leave with Nate. I couldn't wait to put him to bed tonight, taking as much time as I wanted to read him a story, knowing I didn't have to leave him again.

I watched Jane and Nate passing my things back and forth between themselves, as I stood beside the window, Milo in my arms. My palm travelled gently along the curve of his spine and over the downy fluff on his head and I looked down, finding him staring up at me. There was no fear now. Just an all consuming, powerful and pure love. I couldn't even put into words how much I loved this baby. How had I ever thought otherwise? He was perfect. So very perfect. I felt a tear slip from the corner of my eye, rolling along my nose. It clung to the tip for a few seconds, before falling, landing in the centre of Milo's forehead. I wiped it away with the pad of my thumb and looked up to find both Nate and Jane watching me.

"It will get easier, love," Nate said, his voice gentle.

I nodded, swallowing thickly. "I know. At least, I hope so." I gave a tiny shrug, feeling the tears well in my eyes again. The doctor had said that crying was a good thing. It meant I was able to tune into my emotions, that I wasn't numb to the world around me.

It was all part of healing. *It was okay to be sad.* I wasn't sure I had ever been told that before.

I cleared my throat and offered a weak smile. "I just can't see how I will ever be able to forgive myself for all the terrible things that went through my head. You would hate me if you knew the extent of it all. And the things I did. What I *could* have done." I broke off, shaking my head. It was too awful to even consider.

"I know it's hard, Meg," Nate said, his forehead creasing. "But you have to let go of that guilt. It wasn't your fault. If anything, it was mine. I should have been more aware. Asked more questions. Not a minute passes that I don't think about all the signs I missed. I play that day over and over in my head. What if I'd never come home for lunch? What if I'd lost you… them? You can't blame yourself, Meg. It was my fault things got as bad as they did."

"And mine," Jane said, gripping my nightgown midway through folding it. Her eyes were glistening with unspilled tears. "I knew something was wrong. Badly wrong. But I was so afraid. I didn't know what to do. I'm so sorry I didn't fight harder, Megan. I was worried I was seeing things that weren't there. Building it up. I couldn't be positive, you see, and I didn't want to risk losing you. All of you. I couldn't bear the thought of you cutting me out, thinking I was just a meddlesome old woman. I'm so sorry I didn't swallow my fears and do more."

"No, Mum, don't say that," Nate said, placing a big arm around her shoulders, squeezing tight. "You tried. Every day you tried to get me to see what was happening right in front of me." He sighed and threw me a crooked smile, though it didn't reach his eyes. He looked so crestfallen. "I guess I was just so sure it would all resolve itself. It was stupid of me."

"No," I said. "You did all you could. Both of you. It was *me*. I'm the one who cracked up. I mean, I truly believed that this tiny, innocent baby, was evil. That he had some awful plan to destroy the world or something. I was scared of my own son. It sounds so ridiculous now, but it felt so real at the time. I can still remember how it felt every time I held him, every time I looked at him. It's surreal, like remembering back to another life. It's as if I'm holding on to someone else's memories. Because now, I can see how insane those fears were." I held Milo closer as if I could protect him from the terrible things that past version of myself had thought of him. "I still don't really understand it, but neither of you were to blame. Just me."

"No."

I turned towards the sound of the new voice behind me. Doctor Parkins was standing just inside the room, shaking his head slowly. "I'm sorry?"

He gave a soft smile. "I said no." He shrugged, putting his hands in his trouser pockets and fixing me with a look of immense kindness. "People always look to place blame when they've been through a trauma. It's a distinctly human thing to do. To decide who is at fault. Who to direct their anger towards. It can help some people to understand what's happened to them. To give them something to focus on, you know? And if it helps the healing process, then I see no problem with that. By all means, find someone you can blame. But make that target someone who you never have to see again. Make it the doctor who missed the signs. The midwife who could have filed a report. Not each other. Your family. And certainly not yourselves. Don't turn that anger inwards and let it make you bitter and fearful."

He looked to Nate and Jane still standing by the bed, listening intently to his every word. "Right now, you as a family need to lean on one another more than ever before. And to do that, to be vulnerable and honest and open about your struggles, you need forgiveness. Not only for each other, but for yourselves too. Because the truth is, nobody is to blame. It's *not* your fault, Megan. Or yours, Nate. Or yours either, Jane. Postpartum Psychosis is *rare*. So rare that most of my patients who develop it, have never heard of the condition before they wind up admitted to my ward. *Of course* symptoms were missed. You had no idea what to look out for. And Megan, you were in the midst of a serious mental illness and had no idea what was happening to you. It's not anybody's fault that you developed this. Not even your own."

"But I could have killed him. I came so close."

"I know," he gave a grave nod. "And I've seen patients in here with the very same condition, who weren't so lucky as you. Those who never got that moment of clarity to stop them in their tracks. Women who have hurt their children, badly, and yes, those who have even killed their babies in the hight of delusion. You yourself nearly took your own life. You know that your mind was not your own during that time. Those women all did what they did because like you, they were ill, Megan. Even those women who killed their babies can't be blamed. It wasn't their fault. To their minds, they were living with demons, monsters, they were doing the only thing they could to survive in the world they believed they were living in. None of them were violent women. None of them would have laid a finger on their children had they been well. But they weren't in control. And it wasn't their fault."

A choked sob came from behind me and I spun around to see Jane stuffing her fist in her mouth, tears streaming down her pale, clammy cheeks. "Jane?" I asked, moving forward with the intention of hugging her.

She shook her head. "Excuse me," she managed to splutter. Then she darted past me and ran out of the room and down the corridor.

"I'll go," Nate said, his brow furrowing in concern.

"No, please. Let me," I said.

He nodded slowly. "If you're sure?"

"I am." I placed Milo gently in his arms, pleased to find that I missed his presence instantly, then turned to face Doctor Parkins.

"I'm sorry," he muttered, clearly embarrassed. "I spoke out of turn."

"No, you didn't, and it was something I think we all needed to hear. Thank you," I said, meaning every word.

Nate nodded in agreement. "Yes, thank you, Doctor. For all you've done for our family. You've put us back together again."

"I merely did my job," he said. "But it has been a pleasure to see you return to full health, Megan. I'll leave you to get on." He left the room and I followed him out, heading in the opposite direction to go and find my mother-in-law.

Chapter Thirty-One

Megan

I walked quickly along the now familiar corridor, its large windows looking out over the secure courtyard garden where I'd spent countless hours over the past four weeks since being transferred to the mother and baby unit. When I'd first been admitted to the main psychiatric unit, I'd been confined to the indoors, not trustworthy enough to be given permission to venture outside for fear that I might hurt myself. *Suicide watch,* they had called it.

It was mind boggling to me now, that I had ever considered such a thing. To leave my children without a mother. To leave Nate to deal with the aftermath and pick up the pieces, alone and grieving. It was such a selfish thing to even consider. But it wasn't my fault, I reminded myself, Doctor Parkins' words still fresh in my mind. I didn't quite believe them, not yet. But he was right about needing to move forward. And if being kinder to myself would help my family to find a way back to each other and heal, I would try my hardest to let that message of forgiveness sink in. I would do anything to make things better.

I scoured the courtyard garden through the window, catching a bright flash of fuchsia pink in the far corner, shielded by the holly bush. The red berries were in full bloom now and I reminded myself to make time to teach Toby about which berries to avoid when we got back home. I had missed so much.

I was desperate to get back to the mundane, ordinary routines and conversations from which I'd derived so much pleasure before it had all gone wrong. I wanted to take his hand and show him how to pick the ripe Autumn olives from the tree in the back garden. I'd missed my chance this year. They would all be mulch on the lawn by now. But next year, we would go out together, ceramic bowl in hand, choosing the best ones from each bunch. Then I would show him how to make tart, tasty jam from the nutritious little berries.

I wanted to sit at our little craft table, winding willow twigs into a wreath, not beautiful, but made with love and joy, to place on our front door so that

Nate could see when he came home that he was walking into a place of warmth. Somewhere safe, where he didn't have to feel afraid. It was a relief to know that I would be home in time for Christmas. That I hadn't spoiled that for everyone too.

Not your fault. Not your fault.

It would be a slow process for that message to sink in. But I wouldn't stop trying. I pushed the door to the courtyard open, reeling at the frigid bite to the air, wrapping my cardigan tighter around my body. I glanced over my shoulder, wishing I'd thought to pick up our coats. It was too late for that now, but as I cast a wistful look behind me, I saw the linen closet, its door ajar, and with a relieved smile I rushed over to it, grabbing two blankets from the neatly folded pile before heading outside.

I walked quietly, aware of the soft sound of crying coming from where Jane sat, her head in her hands, her wide back heaving as she sucked in steadying breaths. Wordlessly, I moved closer, unfolding one of the blankets and laying it across her shoulders before wrapping the other one around myself. I'd lost so much weight in the two months since Milo had been born, forgetting to eat for days on end whilst I was ill, and putting up a fight at every meal for the first few weeks in hospital.

Now, my collarbone and shoulder-blades jutted out and a fine, downy fur covered my back and my face. The nutritional team had said that my body had gone into starvation mode. The fine hair had sprung up in it's attempt to protect my organs in the absence of fat. It was startling to see my own reflection, to notice all the changes that had occurred in my body in such a short space of time. I'd been put on a strict meal-plan to follow to help me get back up to a healthy weight, but in the meantime, I was susceptible to the cold in a way I'd never been before.

I sat down on the wooden bench beside Jane, and she looked up, staring out over the courtyard, her tears still flowing fast. I took her hand, holding it between mine, squeezing it. "What's upsetting you so much?" I asked softly. She shook her head, remaining silent. I breathed in through my nose, steeling myself. "Jane... I haven't apologised to you yet. And it isn't because I'm not sorry, either. It's because I just haven't been able to find the words." She continued to stare out at the barren garden, ravished by winter and I was glad that she didn't turn to look at me. It made it easier to speak. "I haven't forgotten the way I treated you, and yes, I was ill, but words hurt, and I know you were scared you would lose us. It must have been awful for you, Jane. And I'm so sorry you got the brunt of it."

"You don't have to apologise to me. I'm not angry with you."

"I don't know what we would do without you. It's hard to fathom what was going on in my mind back then. I know it doesn't make any sense, but I really thought you wanted to take my children from me."

"I did."

The admission was barely a whisper. So quiet it could have been lost in the breeze if I hadn't been listening so closely. A sick wave of fear washed over me as I wondered if I was once again falling victim to the delusions that had made me become someone entirely different. I couldn't go through that. Not again. Jane squeezed my hand and I stared at her. "What did you say?" I whispered.

She sighed. "I *did* want to take them. You weren't imagining that part. But it wasn't for the reasons you thought." She looked into my eyes, her expression serious. "Megan, I *knew*. I knew what was happening to you, and I was so terrified for those boys. I wanted to save them from you, but I didn't know how."

"How long did you know?"

"From very early on I suspected." She took a deep breath and let go of my hand, pulling the blanket tightly around herself.

"How?" I asked, though I had a sudden realisation that I knew what she was going to say. "Jane... did this... did it happen to you? With Nate?"

She looked at me, fresh tears in her eyes and I saw the truth. "Yes," she said quietly. "It happened to me."

Chapter Thirty-Two

Jane

I couldn't believe what I was about to do. The thought of it made my mouth dry, my pulse roaring in my ears. I was glad I was sitting down. I'd kept the secrets of my past locked up for so long, I wasn't sure I even knew how to let them out. But along with the trepidation coursing through my body, I also felt ready to burst with the truth. *This* was the time. I had planned to take it to my grave, but now I had an opportunity to spill my soul to another person, and I would not let it slip through my fingers.

I slipped my hand inside my turquoise leather handbag and pulled out my purse. Pausing, I looked around at Megan beside me on the bench, our eyes meeting. She was pale and silent as she waited for me to speak. With a wave of nausea, I swallowed down the acrid taste of bile in my throat, unclipped the clasp of my matching turquoise leather purse and pulled out an old, square photograph faded at the edges from years of handling. Without a word, I handed it to her, watching her brow crease as she looked down at the photo, handling it gently.

"But... I don't understand?" She brought the photograph closer, her eyes widening in shock. "Oh." It seemed to click all at once. "Oh, Jane!"

"Yes." I took the picture back, running my fingertip over the image. A tiny baby girl, dressed in a soft white gown adorned with dainty pink flowers, a shock of blonde hair on her head and a sweet little Alice band resting around her crown. She had been a beautiful baby. An *angel*, her father had called her.

I plucked a second photograph from inside my purse and handed it over. "That's me," I said wryly. "Quite a difference to nowadays. I doubt anyone who knew me back then would even recognise me now." The photograph had been taken when the baby was just a day old. The stranger, a version of myself I could hardly recall, sat frozen in time, laughing into the camera as she sat in a rocking chair. My hair had been just a shade darker than the baby's golden tresses. Very different from the mousy brown I kept it coloured in now.

"I was petite back then," I murmured, more to myself than to Megan, though I saw her cover her mouth with her hand as she realised she was looking at her fat old mother-in-law. I couldn't blame her. She had never seen me as anything else. Neither had Nate, really. "My husband, John, said he didn't believe I could have had a baby. That I must have had a cushion stuffed up my jumper and pinched a nipper from the mother and baby ward for me to spring back so quickly. He did like to tease."

"I never knew you had a daughter," Megan murmured. "I always thought Nate was an only child."

"He doesn't know. Not many people do."

She stared at me, not unkindly, but with a thousand questions in her eyes. I swallowed, unsure if I could go on. It all seemed so fresh. So raw. Even after more than five decades. "What was her name?"

"Susan. We had planned to call her Suzy, for short." I slipped the photograph carefully inside my purse and slid it into my handbag.

"Will you tell me?" she asked softly.

"I'll try." I chewed my lower lip, trying to figure out how to start. The silence stretched on, but Megan waited quietly, giving the impression there was no hurry. I was grateful for that. Finally, I spoke.

"It happened three years before I had Nate. I was just eighteen. John and I had met on the market, he had a little stall selling tools, hardware type things, and we'd got chatting when I'd gone on an errand for my dad to pick up a bag of screws. It all happened so fast. We fell in love and married just four months later. It was like that, back then. At least, it was in my circles. I never did the whole hippy thing, not that I wanted to, but even if I had, my parents were far too conservative to let anything like that happen," I shrugged.

"I was lucky as it was that they didn't put up any objections to John. Our families were from different walks of life and I thought they might be snobbish about it. They surprised me by accepting him from the very first day they met. I got pregnant right away, maybe even on the wedding night and I couldn't have been more happy. It felt like life was coming together for me. I was a woman, no longer a child. I was going to be a mother. God, it felt like we were untouchable. Like nothing could go wrong. We were happy, Megan. And so very in love," I said with a wistful sigh, the memories still so bright in my mind.

"Susan... Suzy, she was to be the start of our family and we dreamed of the future with such innocent hope. We would lie in bed, night after night watching her roll and stretch in my belly, making up stories about who she would be, which of us she would take after. I wanted her. I did. I never once wished I could go back to being that young unmarried girl with all her options still wide open. I was ready. At least, I thought I was."

Megan nodded, tears already streaming down her gaunt face as she listened to me talk. "And?" she asked softly. "When she arrived?"

I stared straight ahead, my hands finding the edge of the bench, gripping the smooth wood tightly beside my thighs. "I think you know," I whispered. "It happened a little differently for me. More quickly. One minute I was fine. Blissfully happy. She wasn't more than forty-eight hours old when it all changed." I swallowed the lump that had wedged itself deep in my throat, squeezing my eyes tightly shut. I couldn't bear to look at her as I said the words that had to come next.

"I have never tried to explain this to anyone, bar John, because I knew they wouldn't understand. They would despise me, the way I have despised myself since then. But I know you will understand. You've experienced it." I took a deep breath, still not able to look at her.

"The hallucinations came on fast. The most terrible, terrible things, Megan. I still remember every detail now. John was no help. He was just like Nate. Didn't want to see the severity of what was going on beneath his own roof. He was barely home during the daytime, busy with the market stall." I bit my lip, sick with the memories that were as fresh as they had ever been. "It happened when she was five days old. Just *five* days. That was it. Her whole life. I thought she was being attacked, you see. Wild dogs. I can still hear the sounds, their teeth ripping into her. It was so real.

I – I thought I was fighting them off. Saving her," I sobbed, my voice thin and reedy now as I struggled to get the words out. "She was so small, so tiny, I really believed she was being hurt... I didn't realise it was *me* hurting her," I gasped.

"John came home and found... he found..." I broke off, gasping at the horror of reliving that awful day. Megan reached for my hand, prizing it from the edge of the bench, squeezing it tightly. I looked at her face, seeing the empathy in her eyes as she silently urged me on. "He found me shaking her," I said, matter of factly. "I don't know how long it had gone on for, but she was cold and stiff when he managed to prize her from my arms."

"Oh, Jane! Oh my goodness."

I nodded. "My poor little girl," I whispered. "I was supposed to keep her safe, and instead I did *that* to her."

"Shit," Megan said, slumping back against the bench, her hand still around mine. She closed her eyes, tears escaping from beneath her tightly shut eyelids, her breath coming rapidly. When she opened her eyes, she shook her head. "Jane, I can't believe you've been holding onto that all this time. And you were so young. It must have been terrifying."

I nodded again. "Yes. It was."

She was silent for a moment. "What happened to you? After?" she asked. "Oh, please don't say you went to prison?"

"No... worse than that. I – we, covered it up. Well, it was mostly John. He realised by then what he was dealing with, how insane I'd actually gone, though of course he had no idea why I'd suddenly snapped. If it's considered a rare condition now, you can imagine how unknown it was back in the sixties. We had no google. No NHS Direct on the phone. There was no way we could hide the fact that I'd lost my mind. I was still hallucinating, even after she was gone," I said, my voice filled with the self loathing I'd kept hidden for so long.

"John dealt with everything. It was different back then. Everything is so thorough now, it would all come out in a matter of days. But back then, it was different. Small village mentality still meant something. We kept our business, *our* business, stuck together and didn't involve outsiders. John reported it as cot death. It had been in the news a few months before, some new discoveries into why some babies simply go to sleep and never wake up, that ended up snowballing into the SIDS campaigns we know today. It was at the forefront of everyone's minds, so I suppose that was why he grasped at it. He just said she'd gone down for her nap and that I'd found her dead when I went to get her up, just like all those other poor babies. And the police chief of our local station was a good friend of his. John had been to school with his younger brother and spent half his childhood round their house for dinner. He was so cut up about it on John's behalf, and mine too, that it was all put to bed quickly without a fuss. No inquest, no questions asked."

Megan frowned. "Small village?"

"That's right. We didn't always live in Brighton, we moved here a year before Nate was born. I know Nate thinks I grew up here, but his father and I grew up in the countryside. A little village just outside

Salisbury, where everyone knew everyone. It was why we moved after... after Suzy was gone. I couldn't bear seeing their pity when I knew I didn't deserve an ounce of it."

"It wasn't your fault."

"So the wise Doctor Parkins said."

"But, you must have seen a doctor too? To get well again?"

"Not right away. John was ashamed, I think. That and frightened of what would happen to me if the truth came out. He took a week off work, not that we could afford it, but there was no other option – I couldn't be left alone. He tried his best to help, but I think he made things worse."

"What did he do?"

"Locked me in the bedroom. He took everything out, with the exception of a bare mattress. He feared for my safety too, you see. But being locked up like that, not being able to find my baby or remember why she was missing, it magnified everything. He was only trying to help, but in truth, it had the opposite effect. After a week, I was no better, unsurprisingly. He couldn't take any more time away from the stall and I think he knew just how out of his depth he was. Half the time, I was launching myself at him, convinced that *he'd* taken my baby from me. I'm sure it was a very difficult time for him. He was grieving for his child and had nobody to turn to, no one he could confide in. I don't know all the ins and outs, but he made some calls, blamed it on losing the baby and I was taken into the mental health hospital – they called it the asylum in the village. I was eventually treated for post traumatic stress and a nervous breakdown. They thought the grief had caused my symptoms," I shrugged.

"I expect I would have recovered more quickly if they'd realised what they were dealing with, but I'm glad they didn't. I wasn't ready to be well again. To face what I'd done. Coming to my senses and realising what had happened, what I had done to my sweet little baby, was the most awful, sickening experience of my life. It took years before I stopped trying to kill myself. But, in truth, I never have. Not entirely. I swapped pills for overeating and have never, not for one minute stopped trying to punish myself for what I did to my poor baby. That was why Doctor Parkins' words hit me so hard today. I couldn't believe he was condoning those women. Women like me."

"And me."

"No! You stopped yourself, Megan. I didn't. I was too weak."

"No, Jane. You were too *ill*. There's a difference. And he's right. Neither of us could help the things we did."

"It doesn't change anything though, does it? It won't bring her back."

"No," she whispered. "It won't."

We sat in silence, hand in hand, lost in our own thoughts. The wind whipped around us, bitingly cold, and I took comfort in it's punishing presence.

"Jane?" Megan said. "What about Nate? Tell me about having him. Weren't you afraid?"

I felt the corners of my mouth twitch as I pictured him, my beautiful son, the robust, smily little baby that had come into my life in a burst of sunshine. He'd been so different from his sister, right from the start and that had been a blessing. It had meant I never considered him a replacement for my quiet, delicate little Suzy. He was very much his own person, and I loved him all the more for it.

"I suppose I never got over the fact that I'd been a mother and had it come to an abrupt end before I really got to experience it. My mind recovered – from the psychosis, at least, but as the years passed, I became obsessed with the idea of having another baby. It was all I thought about, and I knew, if I could just get John to agree, I would have a chance to finally break out of that awful limbo I remained trapped inside. A chance to redeem myself. But John would not agree. He was so scared. Angry too, that I would suggest it. He didn't think I deserved a second chance at motherhood, and I can't blame him for that. Not after what he saw. In a way, it was even worse for him than it had been for me, because he had been in his right mind through it all. He had to live with himself, knowing that he had ignored the signs. He forced me to go on the pill and wouldn't touch me without using a condom."

"So, how did you – ?"

"*You've* been broody, Megan. You know what it feels like. It's an insanity of its own. All you can focus on is getting pregnant, finally feeling the swell and stretch as that tiny being grows inside you. I would wake in the night and imagine that the weight in the crook of my arm, was my baby, rather than that of the pillow which had shifted out of place. I would wrap my arms around sofa cushions while John was at work, rocking them back and forth as I stood in the middle of my living room, singing lullabies, telling fairy-tales. I was desperate. And when you're desperate, you can do things that stretch the boundaries of right and wrong," I admitted.

"I stopped taking the pill. And I poked holes through the condom packets with a fine sewing needle. I make no apology. John and I had been broken from the moment I killed our daughter. He never forgave me, never loved me after that. I was nothing more than a wife of convenience. There to cook his dinners and satisfy his urges in the bedroom. And he hated that I'd gained weight. He would get up from the bed when he'd finished and he would look at me with pure disgust, like he couldn't believe he'd lowered himself to sleeping with someone like me. You saw, I was pretty when he first met me. I was fashionable, at least by the standards in our village, and I took care of myself. He hated the way I started dressing. I always thought these dresses were motherly, homely," I smiled, fingering the soft cotton of my hem. "And when I wore them, I felt like the woman I wanted to be. John didn't like it. Said I looked frumpy and old fashioned. That I didn't have the figure to pull off the look," I grimaced, remembering how mean he had become towards the end of our marriage.

"I'd always known he could have any woman he wanted. He was a good looking man, funny, kind. The whole package to begin with. I ruined that. He was nothing but the pretty shell by the end. The nights of him climbing into bed with me grew further and further apart and I knew it was only a matter of time before he found someone else to take to bed. Time was running out, so I did what I needed to do to get the baby I so desperately wanted. I don't regret it."

"Wow," Megan breathed.

"I know. Quite the story of deception." I gave a wry smile. "Of course, When he found out I was expecting, there was Hell to pay. He demanded I get an abortion. Said he would never be able to trust me alone with his child. I was scared too. Terrified, actually. But we were prepared at least. And as it turned out, I had nothing to worry about. I wish I could say that the days following Nate's birth were the happiest of my life, and in a way, they were. But they were bitter-sweet too. A reminder of what should have been with my sweet Suzy. I threw myself into being a good mother to Nate. It was as if I could make up for what I'd done if I got it just right. If I never let him down, even once. Of course, motherhood doesn't work like that. It's impossible not to fail. But when that happened, I would just try again, even harder. Go that extra mile," I flashed her a knowing smile.

"And yes, I'm fully aware that as mothers go, I can be a little intense. Maybe you can understand why I'm overbearing at times, now that you know my story?"

She nodded, smiling back. "And... Nate's father?" she asked. "I already know there was no happy ending for the two of you."

I shook my head. "No. Sadly not. The love we had once shared was gone. After Suzy, he became someone quite different. I didn't just kill my baby. I killed him too. The John that had been there was gone, replaced by something bitter and angry. I never blamed him, of course. Anyone would react that way. He stayed long enough to be sure I wouldn't hurt Nate. But I'm not sure he ever let himself really love his son. That part of him was just gone, broken. He left when Nate was just eighteen months old. Said he couldn't look at me pretending to be the perfect mother one moment longer. I didn't put up a fight. Life was easier without him around to cast his shadow of bitterness. He'd been a constant reminder of my actions."

"Money was a worry, without his support and I feared how we would cope. But as it happens, John went home, back to the village we'd grown up in and word got back to my parents that he'd left me and the baby in the lurch. To his credit, he let the shame be loaded on his shoulders. Protected me. My dad, bless him, sent me money for years, just enough to get by and then when he and mum died, I bought my house from the sale of theirs. Gosh, I'm so sorry, Megan, I'm rambling, aren't I?" I said suddenly, realising just how long we'd been sitting, huddled in blankets in the freezing cold.

It had been cathartic to let it all come out, after keeping my secrets trapped inside for so long. "Nate will be worrying about us and Toby and Milo will be getting hungry," I said, standing up. "I'm sorry for unloading all that on you. You have enough on your plate right now – "

"Don't be silly," Megan said, rising from her spot on the bench too. "You have no idea how much it means to me that you felt safe enough to share it with me. I feel like I understand you so much better now, Jane." She leaned forward, wrapping me in a tight hug. "It must have been so hard, watching me descend into the same thing. Brought back so many awful memories for you."

"It wasn't easy. But it's helped me to start thinking about what happened a little differently. Logically, I can see now that it wasn't my fault. I didn't intend to hurt her. I loved her so much. I was just lost. As you were. But it will take some time for me to absorb that message and really believe it."

"For me too."

I nodded. "Don't tell Nate, okay? Not yet. One day, if the time is right, I'll tell him myself. But not yet, okay?"

She nodded. "Okay," she agreed softly. "It's your story to tell."

"Thank you," I whispered, feeling closer to her than I ever had before. She was my family. Megan, Nate and those two precious boys. And all things considered, I was very lucky.

"Come on. Let's go back inside. It's time we left this place for good," Megan smiled. I followed her in, knowing that from now on, life would be easier. Suzy would be in my heart until it stopped beating, maybe even after that. I would never forget her. But maybe, in time, I would learn to forgive myself for the things I had done.

Epilogue

Megan

Toby squealed, bouncing up and down on his tiptoes, his hands balling into fists at his sides as Nate fished around under the Christmas Tree. He pulled out a large, rectangular shaped box wrapped in blue paper and placed it on the carpet. "There you go, Tobes," he grinned, winking in my direction. I screwed up my face in mock displeasure, giving into the smile which was trying to break free. The nickname no longer irritated me. Not a bit. If there was one lesson I'd learned this year, it was how to let the little things go.

I watched with pleasure as Toby squatted down, opening the wrapping paper slowly, methodically, his chubby fingers sliding carefully beneath the sellotape. His movements were so precise it was almost comical. Weren't toddlers notorious for their eagerness? Weren't they supposed to rip it off in a flurry of paper and squeals? Toby's eyes shone with excitement as he finally pulled the pristine paper back, revealing a box showing a picture of a child-sized piano. He clapped his hands together, before trying to figure out how to open it. Nate helped him, sliding the perfect replica of a piano from its packaging. "I play it now?" Toby asked, looking at me hopefully.

"Yes, sweetie. I want to hear your beautiful music," I smiled.

"Grandma, too," Jane agreed from her place beside me. She pushed a last morsel of mince pie into her mouth and wiped her sticky fingers on a napkin. "There, I'm ready," she said. Toby needed no further encouragement. The controlled, orderly manner he'd had whilst opening the present was instantly replaced by a frenzied pounding on the keys, filling the room with a tinkling jumble of noise. Jane gave an amused roll of her eyes in my direction. "You might regret that one," she murmured under her breath.

"No," I said, watching him. "I love it. It makes me happy to see him like this." I sighed contentedly, the weight of Milo sleeping in my arms a constant pleasure to me now. Having him close no longer frightened me the way it had when I'd been ill. It was reassuring. Comforting. The way it *should* be between a mother and her baby.

"Here's one for you, Meg," Nate said, kneeling beside the tree, a small package wrapped in silver paper nestled in his palm. He shuffled towards me, placing it in my free hand, his eyes locking with mine for a moment. "Happy Christmas, darling," he said softly.

"Thank you," I replied, feeling my cheeks flush. I felt like a teenager falling in love again every time he looked at me. Giddy with butterflies and excitement for the future. The way he'd decided to just forgive me was something I would be forever in awe of. I'd expected us to argue. To have a layer of bitter resentment between us which we would have to spend the next few years fighting our way through. But my expectations had been proven wrong.

Nate had sat me down that first night after coming home from the unit and we'd had the deepest, most honest talk of our lives, sobbing and holding each other, going over everything we'd feared, everything we'd wished we'd done differently, and everything we were still angry about. I'd confessed my feelings of hurt that he hadn't listened to me, and that despite knowing me better than anyone ever had, he still hadn't seen what was happening right in front of his eyes. He'd admitted that his terror at finding me with my wrist cut had been clouded by blinding rage over the trauma I'd caused to the children. The danger I'd put them in.

We'd cried and talked and apologised and offered forgiveness long into the night, and somehow, our willingness to be raw and honest with one another had helped. It had changed things for the better.

We'd woken up with a fresh new slate the following morning, and true to his word, Nate had refrained from throwing what I'd done in my face, never once speaking to me with a harsh tone or muttering a nasty comment. I knew in my heart that he had forgiven me. That we had forgiven each other and found our way back to being happy. And though I'd doubted Doctor Parkins' prediction that we would emerge from this stronger than before, I could see now that it was true.

I fiddled with the wrapping paper, trying to open the present with my one free hand, the other still clasped around Milo, and with a laugh I realised it was impossible. Turning to Jane, I smiled. "Will you hold Milo for me?"

She nodded, sliding him from my arms, settling his sleeping body against her chest and leaning back against the cushions. Everything had changed between us now, too. We were close. Closer than we had ever been. I carried her deepest secrets with me and I understood her in a way I had never been able to before. I could see that her desperation to be close to us, involved in the children's lives, was not a challenge to my own position, nor a way of bringing them over to her side, stealing their love from me. She had never wanted to take over. I could see that now. But being surrounded by a loving family was necessary to her. It made her feel worthwhile. Needed. Whole. It was healing for her. I understood that now.

She had given up her job without a second thought, so that she could support us through my hospital stay, and where I might have once considered that presumptuous and suffocating, now I was simply grateful to have her in our lives. There had never been any question of cutting her out when I came home.

We'd fallen into an easy pattern where she would come round after lunch most days, stopping to play or taking the boys out, either for a walk or back to her house to play there. She would bring them back to me a couple of hours later, after I'd had chance to rest and catch up on housework, and we would all eat dinner together. Jane seemed happier than I'd ever seen her and I was glad. She deserved it after the trauma she'd been through. Her and her poor little Suzy. I squeezed her hand, my eyes meeting hers, and she nodded, understanding passing between us.

Toby stood up from his place by the piano, toddling over and climbing up between us on the sofa. "Open it, Mama," he said, pointing to my present.

"Okay," I smiled. I slipped my thumb beneath the tape, sliding a blue velvet jewellery box from the shining, silver paper. "Do you want to help me?" I asked Toby, grinning as his face turned serious, concentrating on the task. He lifted the lid of the box and sat back triumphantly. A beautiful, silver bracelet sat on the blue satin cushion and I reached into the box, lifting it out. Two swirling charms were clasped to it and my brow creased as I held them up to the light. "Is it...?"

"Baby hair," Nate answered softly. His finger touched the glass bead with swirls of light brown set into its resin. "This is a lock of Toby's hair from when he was born. And this," he said, touching the darker bead, "is Milo's. I thought it would be a nice idea... you know, so you could keep them with you wherever you are."

Tears of pure joy sprang to my eyes. "It's beautiful," I whispered. "Oh, Nate, I love it," I cried, holding out my wrist so he could put it on for me.

"I wanted it to serve as a reminder of who you are. How loved you are," he said, sitting back on his heels. I smiled at him through a veil of tears, casting my gaze around at my home, the beautiful decorations I'd made by hand with Toby by my side, Milo snoozing in my lap. I saw the ease in which Jane sat with Milo, the trust in Toby's eyes as he looked up at me, watching me with fascination. I'd been lost. So lost. And I'd come so frighteningly close to tipping right over the edge. Of destroying something so beautiful I couldn't even put words to it. My family. But I knew I was one of the lucky ones. I'd been given the help to move forward. To keep living.

The days weren't always perfect. There were times when a dark cloud hovered over me and I couldn't seem to shift it. Visits from the social worker we'd been assigned, where I had to bite my tongue and accept their intrusion into my home, my children's lives. Memories that could be forgiven but never erased. But we had made it past the stormiest times and out the other side. We had something that couldn't be bought or faked. A loving family. A happy home. And I wasn't ever going to take that for granted.

The End.

About This Story

I'm writing this after the flurry of Christmas celebrations, surrounded by new toys the children have already fallen in love with and drinking a hot cup of tea from the sanctuary of my bedroom – I still haven't got to grips with using my proper desk in my office to write. It continues to bring me back to memories of enforced schoolwork, a sure-fire way to kill my creative buzz. The novel is complete, edited and ready to go out into the world and finally, I feel as if I can breathe.

Several of my early readers told me that this was a difficult story to read, because of the emotions involved and the rawness of Megan's despair as she descended into psychosis. I'm sure you can imagine, if it was hard to read, it was even more of a challenge to write. The words come easily for me, but locking yourself away for hours on end to delve into a character whose mind is failing her, is an intense experience.

Frequently I would emerge from a day of scribbling away, to join my family for dinner in a cloud of confusion and volatile emotions. Going deep into that mindset was intense. And often frightening, because as a mother, this is the stuff of nightmares and yet for some, this is their reality.

The idea for 'The Things You Cannot See' first came to me after clicking on a YouTube documentary and watching in fascination as women described their experiences with the condition. The fear that they couldn't keep their babies safe, or worse still, the belief that their baby was dangerous somehow. Sadly, one mother who had been diagnosed too late, had smothered her baby during his nap, and I was struck by the horror of her situation, the guilt she would carry with her for the rest of her life, all because her symptoms were missed.

Creating awareness for Postpartum Psychosis, wasn't my primary objective when writing this book. I wrote it for the love of the story, and the emotions I wanted to explore within the characters. However, if this book helps more people to learn about this rare and dangerous condition and to seek treatment as a result, then I consider that a success.

If you enjoyed this story I would be very grateful if you could leave a review on Amazon for me. They make such a huge difference to me as an author and help new readers to find my books.

And if you want to be the first to know about the

next book I release, pop over to www.samvickery.com and sign up for my free reader list where you'll get all the latest news and no spam!

Sam Vickery

Also from Sam Vickery

One More Tomorrow

Chapter One

I can't remember a time in my childhood when I ever dreamed of being a mother. Whilst my sisters were cooing over their Tiny Tears dolls, rocking their chubby plastic bodies and jamming magic milk bottles into their oddly triangular mouths, I was in the garden digging a hole to Australia, or climbing up the tall oak tree to launch my teddy from the topmost branches, testing out the latest parachute I'd invented out of a paper napkin and a tangled ball of my mother's wool. I was reading about how planets are formed, or making clay sculptures – which I was sure would make me a famous artist. I was busy, and curious and relentless in my thirst for knowledge. Babies did not interest me in the slightest.

Susie next door had one, a dribbly, demanding six month old brother called Davey – runny gravy, I called him behind her back – who I heard squealing and crying through the thin walls of our terraced house every morning before the sun was even up. I would roll over, huffing and grimacing, pulling my pillow hard over my ears as I tried to block out his piercing intrusions. Babies did not let people sleep, I'd deduced from these frequent unwelcome awakenings.

Susie was a typically proud big sister. She would grin indulgently as he knocked over her carefully constructed tower of bricks, not caring that he was rudely interrupting our game, dragging us out of our imagined world of pirates, magic and adventure to wave a chewed rusk in her face. I hated him.

As I lay in my huge, grown up sized bed now with the pre-dawn haze filtering through the sheer blue curtains, Lucas's warm strong back pressed up against my side as he slept, I wondered if that was why I was being punished. If I had brought on my own misery through some sort of wicked karma. My disdain, or at least my disinterest in babies had carried on right up until I turned twenty-eight. I'd managed to come through school, university, marry Lucas and get a job teaching anthropology – a subject I adored – without ever considering the possibility of motherhood. Lucas had been surprised at my certainty that children were not to be on the cards, but he was willing to box up that dream if it meant keeping me. Everything had been just as it should have been. Life was ticking by, following my carefully crafted plan. Everything was perfect. Until my twenty-eighth birthday.

There had been too much vodka for both of us. Laughter, fumbling in the dark, wrapped together in a tangle of limbs and lust. A torn condom that went unnoticed until it was too late. A shared glance of panic and bewilderment in the morning that followed. And then, though I held on to my sense of normal, my orderly, controlled reality, though I grasped onto it with all my might, there was nothing I could do to take back that night. In a few moments of reckless passion everything had changed.

Suddenly, those doors which had been bolted shut, the lock rusted and unmoving, had been burst open with an explosion that shattered them into tiny little splinters. We had done something that could not be undone, and all at once a whole new path lay before us, shining with possibility. And for no reason I could fathom, without reason or logic, I just knew, *I knew* that I had to follow it. As soon as I realised a heart beat other than my own was fluttering inside my womb, depending on me for its very existence, I knew. I was going to be a mother. I wanted it more intensely than I had ever wanted anything. I felt fierce and strong and primal. This was what I was meant to do, I knew it.

Except it wasn't.

Eleven weeks. Eleven precious, wonderful weeks. That's how long I managed to keep him alive. Don't ask me how, but I knew it was a boy. My son. Eleven weeks he grew and developed and changed me in ways that could never be erased. And then, in a wave of crippling cramps and clotted blood, he was gone. My son. My angel.

After he left me, I found I was no longer complete. I was not the person I had been before, I was something new, something empty and lost. I couldn't go back now that I had seen what could be. I couldn't forget how it had felt to be a mother, to be needed so deeply, to love so hard. I couldn't undo it.

Lucas stirred beside me and I glanced through tear fogged eyes at the small silver clock on the bedside cabinet. It had been my mother's and hers before that, and every time I looked at it I remembered with vivid clarity how it had felt to wake up in her big bed as a small child, her tanned arm slung loosely over my torso, the shining silver clock ticking quietly beside us.

She would wake groggy and grumpy, and I would have to cajole her into the day, convince her it really was morning time, though she would groan and refuse to open her eyes. "Just five more minutes, my darling. It's still dark," she would moan from under the covers. I would huff and sigh and fidget impatiently beside her as she ignored me, trying to get a few more precious moments of rest. Then, as if a switch had been flicked on, she would suddenly be ready, throwing the blankets to the ground and grabbing me tight, pulling me in for a hug and kissing me all over my face. I would squeal and try to get away, though really I loved it. She would jump out of bed singing at the top of her voice, her grumpiness forgotten and buried, at least until the next morning. The clock filled me with nostalgia and sadness, yet I refused to part with it. Painful though they were, the memories of my mother were all I had left. They were better than nothing at all.

Lucas stirred again. I wiped my swollen eyes against the pillowcase, though I knew he would know right away that I'd been crying for hours. That my night had been filled with the endless pacing and wicked nightmares I was fast becoming used to. He always wanted to talk, to get me to tell him every little detail of what was upsetting me. To share the horror of the nightmares, the stories I told myself in the dark quiet hours. It was pointless. He knew that as well as I did, but he kept on trying, pushing, wanting to be there for me, to fix everything. But I couldn't be fixed. He knew that too.

Sometimes Lucas would wake in those dark, lonely

hours, despite my tooth-marked fist, my swallowed, muffled sobs. When he found me in such a state, he would look at me with those big brown eyes glistening in the moonlight with tears he wouldn't shed, his mouth pursed in indecision and sadness. He would take me in his arms and hold me tight until I pretended to fall back to sleep. His comfort never helped. I didn't deserve it. I wanted to suffer alone. I didn't want to see the look of anguish in his eyes.

On this occasion though, I had managed to get a hold of myself before he woke. He would know I'd been crying again, of course. He could always tell. But I wouldn't flaunt it. I never did. Perhaps this morning we could pretend it hadn't happened. I didn't have it in me to talk about it again. At least not yet.

I felt the feather-light touch of his fingertips as they grazed their way through my hair, making their way down my spine. I shivered, instinctively leaning into the security of his warmth. "Good morning," he said, his throat raspy with the after effects of sleep as he nuzzled into my neck.

"Good morning yourself," I replied, my voice falsely bright as I turned to face my husband. He pursed his full lips into a scowl as he caught sight of my puffy eyes and blotchy cheeks, his thick, dark brows furrowing. Even so, I thought, he was still indisputably good looking. His cheekbones were defined and strong. His eyelashes thick, his eyes a pool of rich chocolate. And under the thin sheets, I could make out the defined muscles of his chest and shoulders.

He was a big man at six and a half feet tall. Being only five feet and two measly inches myself, I had always liked that about him. I used to love it when he wrapped me in those massive arms, and made me feel like nothing could hurt me. These days, though, even he couldn't protect me from my pain.

"Rox..." he began, his voice deep and serious. I shook my head.

"Don't, Lucas. Don't. Not today." He twisted his lips again and gave me a long, stern look. Indecision flickered in his eyes. He gave a quick nod and pulled me wordlessly into his chest. I felt myself tense against him as he kissed the top of my head and sighed. Fearing his kindness would only make me start sobbing all over again, I cleared my throat and pulled away, hopping out of bed without meeting his eyes. I could feel his stare burning into my back. I wrapped my cotton dressing gown around my shivering body, pulling my thick dark hair out from under the collar as I headed for the bathroom. "Don't forget, we've got my sisters coming over for lunch today," I told him over my shoulder.

"As if I would forget a visit from the Cormack family," Lucas said, smiling, though it didn't meet his eyes. I paused by the bedroom door, looking at a framed photograph on the wall of my family from last summer. It made me smile every time I saw it, though I never failed to notice the empty space where my mother should have been. My younger sisters, Isabel and Bonnie were identical twins, yet their personalities could not have been more different. Isabel was introverted, sweet, and bordering on genius. We'd expected her to become a physicist, a computer programmer, an entrepreneur, or something equally brilliant and fitting to her intelligence. Yet, she'd surprised us all by choosing to go into social work. She'd actually turned down several promotions because they meant moving away from the personal, one on one duties with the families and children she worked with, to go and push papers around an office instead. Isabel had explained that no pay rise in the world would be enough to pull her away from the people who needed her most. I suspected she thrived on the drama and excitement. Isabel was at her absolute best in a crisis. She was down to earth despite her brilliance, and barely a day went by without us seeing one another.

Bonnie had a polar opposite character to Isabel. Her personality was nothing short of extreme. She was loud, flakey and possibly the most honest person I had ever known. She would say whatever she thought, no matter the consequences. Lucas had once told her she had no filter, to which she'd told him filters were for shifty people and at least he knew what she really thought of him. Thankfully, I had been informed, she liked him. A couple of her exes had not got off nearly so lightly. Though she could be wild and unpredictable, Bonnie was also the most empathetic person I had ever known. She could see right through pretence, right to the source of the pain. A skill she used often, and which proved more than a little annoying when I was trying to pretend I was fine, thank you very much!

As sisters, and as friends we were as close as it gets. Our father had passed away from cancer when the twins were just two. I had been four. And then, we had lost our mother fourteen years later. Now it was just the three of us left from our little family, and the losses had created an unbreakable bond between us. I turned from the photograph, facing Lucas now, and gave him a genuine smile, not the false happy mask I had been pasting on all week. "I know you would never forget," I said. "Thank you." He nodded as he watched me pick up my wash-bag and walk into the bathroom. I could feel his pitying stare burning into my back.

One More Tomorrow is available on paperback and Kindle now.

Printed in Great Britain
by Amazon